# Skin Deep

## Malaika Rose Stanley

Tamarind

SKIN DEEP
A TAMARIND BOOK 978 1 848 53054 6

First published in Great Britain by Tamarind Books,
an imprint of Random House Children's Books
A Random House Group Company

This edition published 2011

1 3 5 7 9 10 8 6 4 2

Copyright © Malaika Rose Stanley, 2011

The Random House Group Ltd supports the Forest Stewardship Council®
(FSC®), the leading international forest certification organization. All our
titles that are printed on Greenpeace approved FSC® certified paper
carry the FSC® logo. Our paper procurement policy can be found at
www.randomhouse.co.uk/environment

MIX
Paper from
responsible sources
FSC® C016897

Set in 12/16pt Minion by Falcon Oast Graphic Art Ltd.

Tamarind Books are published by Random House Children's Books,
61–63 Uxbridge Road, London W5 5SA

www.**kids**at**randomhouse**.co.uk
www.**tamarindbooks**.co.uk
www.**totallyrandombooks**.co.uk
www.**randomhouse**.co.uk

Addresses for companies within The Random House Group Limited
can be found at: www.randomhouse.co.uk/offices.htm
THE RANDOM HOUSE GROUP Limited Reg. No. 954009

A CIP catalogue record for this book is available from the British Library.

Printed and bound in Great Britain by
CPI Bookmarque, Croydon, CR0 4TD

I stared at my reflection in the mirror as I reapplied my lip gloss. Pretty? Yeah, right. People had been saying that for as long as I could remember but it's not true. OK, I'm not a complete minger. I have light-brown skin, which I got from my mum, sprinkled with freckles, which I got from my dad, and amber eyes that are totally random. But I'm short enough to be a munchkin, my boobs are non-existent and if I go out in the rain, I get candyfloss hair! Apart from that, I'm totally stunning. Not.

I turned round and looked up at Bella's face. Her grey eyes were hard and glassy, like marbles. I was completely surrounded by thug girls, but I tried to convince myself that if they were actually going to beat me up I'd have a few cuts and bruises and a broken bone or two by now. I had a last, quick glance at my reflection, popped a Mini-Mint into my mouth and squeezed my way through towards the door.

'Have a nice weekend,' I said sweetly, not sure if I was being brave or brainless.

'You too,' grunted Bella. 'It will be the last one you ever have, because on Monday I'm coming for you. I'm going to make it my mission to make your life hell!'

Also available by Malaika Rose Stanley,
and published by Tamarind Books:

SPIKE AND ALI ENSON

Picture books by Malaika Rose Stanley,
for younger readers:

BABY RUBY BAWLED
MISS BUBBLE'S TROUBLES

Tamarind Books publish multicultural children's books for a
multicultural world. We believe that all children should be
valued for who they are and should live in an environment
which respects their own identity, culture and heritage;
and they should meet people like themselves in the books
they read.

Other fiction from Tamarind Books you might enjoy:

ZILOMBO by S. P. Gates
THE YOUNG CHIEFTAIN by Ken Howard

For Jessica and Sinead,
Cianne and Cara, and Letiya –
*nièces extraordinaires*

# 1

# Friends

It wasn't a rescue mission. I wasn't trying to be a hero. It was Friday afternoon. Time to get the weekend started. All I wanted to do was have a quick pee then roll with Keisha and Ebyan. I raced into the loos, struggling to run with my legs crossed, slipping and sliding across the damp floor. I skidded past a group of girls in our year who were huddled around the wash basins, swerved into a cubicle and slammed the door. I was listening to one of Aaron B's slow jams on my MP3 player, but I pulled off my headphones so I could earwig on the girls outside and suss out what they were up to. I shouldn't have bothered because all I heard was the toxic hiss of Bella Blake's voice.

'What's the matter, Beatrice butter-face?' snarled Bella. 'Are you scared? Are you going to pee yourself?'

'She's going to cry,' said someone else. It might have

been Madison. I wasn't sure because Bella's friends change faster than she changes her knickers! They always stand behind her and agree with everything she says, so they aren't exactly memorable.

'Go on, butter-face. Cry! You'll pee less,' said Bella. 'And the floor is already slimy enough without skanks like you leaking and dripping all over it.'

Some of the other girls snorted with laughter.

'Aaaah,' crowed Bella. 'Does poor likkle baby Betty Bucket want her mummy?'

There was a second or two of silence and then I heard a stifled sob, which I knew had to be coming from Bella's latest victim. Betty – or Beatrice – was in the same year group as the rest of us, but she was one of those odd girls who most people ignored unless they were picking on her. She was dowdy and lanky, and too much of a tomboy for her own good. She had braces and long, straggly mousy-brown hair. I felt a stab of guilt as I realized I didn't even know her real last name.

'Don't blame us,' said the same girl who had spoken before. 'It's not our fault you're so wet. It's not our fault no one likes you.'

'Right,' said Bella. 'And if I were you, I'd want a word with Mummy and Daddy too. They're the reason you're called Betty Bucket!'

'Good one,' sniggered another girl.

I'd heard enough! I yanked open the cubicle door as hard as I could. It swung back on the hinges and smashed into the wall with a massive bang. It was just the effect I was going for. Bella and her motor-mouth friends turned away from Beatrice and gaped at me.

'What the hell is going on?' I yelled, throwing in a few other words which would have got me permanently excluded if any teachers had been around.

'Nothing for you to bother your pretty little head about,' sneered Bella. 'Get lost, Destiny, you nosy cow!'

I aired her and looked at Beatrice. 'Are you OK?'

Beatrice sniffed and stared hard at the floor.

'Go home,' I said, doing my best to sound calm and in control.

Beatrice glanced round at Bella and her bully-girl mates.

'Go on,' I said. 'Go home.'

Beatrice shuffled out. No one tried to stop her. To be honest, I was scared stiff and I wanted to run after her. I had to force myself to stroll over to a sink and wash my hands.

'Why are you sticking your beak in?' said Bella. 'Who asked you?'

'I just don't like seeing you make Beatrice's life a misery.'

'We could always make *your* life a misery instead,' said Bella. 'No one likes you either.'

'Not true,' I said quietly. I fluffed up my mane of soft, reddish-brown curls to hide the shiver that crept along my spine. 'Plenty of people like me.'

'They wouldn't like you if we mashed up your pretty face,' said Bella.

I stared at my reflection in the mirror as I reapplied my lip gloss. Pretty? Yeah, right. People had been saying that for as long as I could remember but it's not true. OK, I'm not a complete minger. I have light-brown skin, which I got from my mum, sprinkled with freckles, which I got from my dad, and amber eyes that are totally random. But I'm short enough to be a munchkin, my boobs are non-existent and if I go out in the rain, I get candyfloss hair! Apart from that, I'm totally stunning. Not.

I turned round and looked up at Bella's face. Her grey eyes were hard and glassy, like marbles. I was completely surrounded by thug girls, but I tried to convince myself that if they were actually going to beat me up I'd have a few cuts and bruises and a broken bone or two by now. I had a last, quick glance at my reflection, popped a Mini-Mint into my mouth and squeezed my way through towards the door.

'Have a nice weekend,' I said sweetly, not sure if I was being brave or brainless.

'You too,' grunted Bella. 'It will be the last one you ever have, because on Monday I'm coming for you. I'm going to make it my mission to make your life hell!'

She started a slow hand-clap and her dollies – the cloned sheep sort – joined in even though I was sure they didn't know what they were applauding.

Outside, I switched Aaron B back on and looked across the playground to where Keisha and Ebyan were propped against the gates, chatting and cracking up. Keisha's navy school skirt and tie were as short as our year tutor would let anyone get away with and her head was covered in an explosion of tiny braids. Ebyan's skirt was floor-length and her head was covered with a matching blue hijab. They were as different as fire and water, but they'd been best friends since nursery and even though Keisha is my cousin I'm still a bit of a tag-along.

Mrs Warsame used to worry that Keisha would be a bad influence on her daughter – but Ebyan is fierce and feisty and no one could ever make her do anything she didn't want to do. It was her own decision to start wearing hijab when we started high school and she dresses traditionally – and stylishly.

She turned round and beckoned to me to hurry up. I sighed with relief, happy my friends were still waiting, and then flinched as I sensed a sudden movement behind me. I whirled round.

'Beatrice!' I gasped. 'I didn't hear you! You scared me!'

'Sorry. I had to make sure you got out of there alive. I wanted to say thank you.'

'No problem,' I said, reluctantly tucking away my MP3 and turning back towards Keisha and Ebyan.

'Really,' said Beatrice, falling into step beside me. 'I don't know what they would have done if you hadn't turned up.'

'Bella is full of it,' I said. 'Small brain, big mouth. All talk and no action.'

'Still,' said Beatrice. 'Thanks.'

'You just need to stand up to her,' I said, sounding more sure than I felt.

'Easy for you to say,' said Beatrice, with a crooked grin that showed off her braces. 'You're not the one she picks on. You're not the one she calls Betty Bucket!'

'True.' I smiled. 'But please, what *were* your parents thinking?'

'My mother is from France – and trust me, Béatrice Buchet sounds much better with a friendly voice and a French accent.'

'Boo-shay,' I repeated, trying it out. 'Nice. But why didn't she call you Monique or Chantelle or something?'

'You think I haven't asked her that about a million times?' said Beatrice gloomily.

We reached the gates.

'At last,' said Ebyan. 'You have been ages. We are growing roots.'

'What's going on?' said Keisha, nodding towards Beatrice.

'A bit of bother with the Bella Blake bullies,' I said.

'That's alliteration,' said Beatrice.

Keisha, Ebyan and I stared at her.

'OK, cuz,' said Keisha after a second. 'You've so done your good deed for the day, but come on now. Let's go.'

I could guess what she was thinking. She didn't want to be seen with *Betty Bucket* in case it reflected badly on her own stunning sense of style and sophistication.

'Don't be like that,' I said. I looked from Keisha to Beatrice and back again. 'All she needs is some re-branding and a makeover.'

'You are both as bad as each other,' said Ebyan. 'Beatrice is not a packet of biscuits or a bottle of cola that needs new packaging and a new name.'

'No! I'm not!' Beatrice's voice cracked and she began to walk away.

'Hang on,' said Keisha, giving Beatrice the once-over – and probably already making plans for the advertising and promotional campaign. 'I'm sorry, OK?'

Beatrice glanced back over her shoulder. She looked anxious – like an abandoned puppy, afraid of being kicked again.

'Bibi!' said Keisha. 'We could, like, call you Bibi – or Bea.'

Ebyan and Beatrice did not look impressed.

'Or Bee!' said Keisha. 'What about Bee?'

I reckon it said a lot about what a beg-friend Bee was for her to forgive Keisha, agree to a new name and walk home with us.

'Could you really do a makeover?' she asked when we reached the corner of Oakville Road and she got ready to leave us.

'Are frogs waterproof? Is Joel Daley-Clarke all that and a bag of chips?' said Keisha, which made my heart miss a beat because as far as I'm concerned, Joel is *my* bag of chips. 'Styling by Ebyan,' continued Keisha. 'Make-up by Destiny, and hair and nails by me!'

'What about tomorrow?' said Bee.

She sounded so desperate, no one could say she wasn't trying hard to make friends. I knew how she felt. I remembered my first few lonely weeks at high school before Mum practically begged Mrs Obodo to let me change tutor groups and I hooked up with Keisha and Ebyan. I felt sorry for her.

'You could all come round to my place tomorrow

8

afternoon,' she went on. 'This is my road. I live at number sixty-two.'

'Not me,' said Ebyan. 'I have to work in the shop on Saturdays.'

'No probs,' said Keisha. 'We can come to the shop for styling after we've done her hair and face.' She turned to Bee. 'Ebyan's mum owns a clothes shop.'

'We sell Somali wedding dresses,' said Ebyan. 'I am happy to give you fashion advice, Bee – but unless you are planning to get married and you need a *dirac* or a *guntiino*, I don't think you will find anything to buy.'

'That's OK. I think I just need a hair and beauty makeover,' said Bee. 'My mum has put me in for Bright Sparks. I only agreed to it because I thought it might cheer her up. She's been depressed ever since Dad left and they got divorced.'

She hesitated, suddenly worried she might have said too much. I was a bit concerned myself, because missing fathers are a touchy subject for Ebyan too. Her dad has a second wife and family in Mogadishu, but she hardly ever mentions it because she doesn't think we would understand.

'Bright Sparks?' I said, trying to make them both feel more comfortable. 'What's that? I've never heard of it.'

'It's a competition,' said Bee. 'Mum found it on the Internet. She reckons it will make me more confident and help me to make friends.'

'Is it a sports event?' said Ebyan. She was probably relieved I'd managed to change the subject so smoothly.

'I wish,' said Bee. 'No. That's why I need help with personal presentation and poise. It's a beauty pageant – but with a twist.'

'No offence, Bee,' said Keisha. She shook her head and rattled her new multi-hoop drop earrings. 'But don't get carried away, like. We're not miracle workers.'

'It's not only about what you look like,' said Bee. She frowned. 'You have to give a speech, and answer questions and showcase your special talent.'

'I'm in!' I said, giving them a twirl and a curtsey. 'I obviously look fantabulous – but I'm also an outstanding musical talent.' I laughed, although I wasn't completely joking. Not about the music anyway. 'Seriously,' I added. 'I could play cello over an Aaron B backing track – classical and R & B fusion. Maybe we should all enter.'

'Not me,' said Keisha. 'I'm happy to help you out but I'm too busy with dance practice to enter myself. I'm still trying to sort out my *pirouette en pointe*.'

'Nor me,' said Ebyan. 'If my mother found out about it, she would not let me near any of you ever again. It's

OK for you three – you are already going to hell!'

Keisha and I fell about. It was an old joke, but the shocked expression on Bee's face made it even funnier.

'No! No way! Not now! Not ever!'

Mum's voice was so loud and screechy, I wondered if my ears were bleeding.

'Why not?' I said quietly so we wouldn't end up having another shouting match.

'Have you seen how much make-up those girls wear?' shrieked Mum. 'And how few clothes?'

'It's not that sort of contest,' I said. I'd already Googled Bright Sparks and checked out the rules on the website before Mum came home from work. 'It's about talent as well as beauty. It's the perfect chance to show off my cello skills. My R & B mixes are banging.'

'Your cello skills wouldn't be the only thing you'd be showing off,' snapped Mum, finally lowering her volume. 'I don't want you fluttering your eyelashes and flaunting your body!'

'But Mum,' I pleaded. 'It's *natural* beauty – no glitzy costumes or big hair and falsies – just ordinary, everyday clothes and a party or prom dress with light make-up. I could wear one of the dresses that Nan sent me. Just have a look.'

'I don't need to look to know it's all about self-absorbed, conceited girls with eating disorders,' said Mum. 'Any girl with brains would have more sense than to enter a contest like that.'

'Are you saying I don't have brains?'

'Of course not,' said Mum. 'That's exactly my point. I don't want you to go through life depending on your looks. I don't want you to make the same mistakes as me. I want you to be better than me.'

Biff, bam, boom! Here we go again! When Mum was young, she'd been a model. She'd been successful too, and quite well-known. She still looks fit but now she dresses like a frump. She reckons that modelling interfered with her education and prevented her from having a proper career. She has a good job as a furniture restorer in an antiques shop in town but she really wanted to be a vet. And now I'm supposed to become a doctor or a lawyer to make up for it!

'Don't worry,' I muttered under my breath, 'I *will* be better than you.'

Mum's supersonic hearing clearly hadn't been affected by all her shouting.

'OK, young lady,' she said sharply. 'This conversation is over! Upstairs. Homework. Now.'

I stomped out of the kitchen. I didn't slam the door

because I'd done enough of that for one day. But I made a silent promise to myself. I wanted to be a professional musician, and Bright Sparks could be my first big break. I was entering the competition. There was nothing Mum or anyone else could do to stop me.

# 2

## Makeover

The next day, after lunch, Keisha and I made our way to Oakville Road. Bee's house had a garage and a front porch cluttered with wellies, fishing rods, skis and skateboards. I checked my reflection in the glass-panelled door, popped a Mini-Mint into my mouth and rang the bell. Bee's mother answered the door. She took one look at us and her face folded into a confuzzled, unwelcoming grimace.

'Yes. Can I help you?'

'Hello, Mrs Boo-shay,' said Keisha in her best meet-the-parents voice.

Mrs Buchet's perfectly plucked eyebrows flew up her forehead and her perfectly manicured hands flew up to her throat. She ran her fingers over her delicate gold necklace and yanked her cardigan tighter. If I didn't know better, I'd say she thought we were going to rob her. I don't know why. It's not like we were dressed in hoodies or balaclavas or carrying concealed weapons! We were both wearing the new fitted sundresses our nan had sent us from the States. Mine was a red and yellow retro print and Keisha's was white with a black trim.

I wondered if we'd forgotten the number and come to the wrong house. Maybe this wasn't Mrs Buchet – although Keisha was already introducing us and obviously didn't share my doubts.

'It's Destiny and Keisha,' she said. 'We've come to see Bee.'

'Bee?' said Mrs Buchet. 'Oh, you mean Béatrice.' She tried to smile but looked like she was sucking lemons. 'Sorry. Please, do come in. She's expecting you.'

I sensed Keisha's irritation, which matched my own, but then Bee barrelled down the stairs. She was so pleased to see us it seemed best not to mention the fact that her mother had blatantly expected her new friends to be white.

'Come up,' said Bee. She skinned her teeth and flashed her braces. 'My brothers have gone camping in Ross-on-Wye with my Uncle Claude so we've got the place to ourselves.'

'Not quite,' said her mother stiffly.

'*Maman*,' said Bee. She spoke a mixture of English and French with a Brummie accent. 'I told you *mes amies* were coming over to do a makeover and you said you were going into town.'

'I've changed my mind,' said Mrs Buchet. 'I think I'm getting a migraine.'

'Don't worry, *Maman*,' said Bee. 'We won't make too much noise.' She skipped up the stairs and we trailed after her.

Bee's room was smaller than mine but everything was perfectly co-ordinated and it was a lot tidier. The window looked out over a long garden. I watched Bee's mother settle into a padded sun lounger on the patio. There were flower borders and a vegetable patch and, at the end of the lawn, a basketball hoop and a football goal.

'How many brothers have you got?' I asked as I turned back to Bee.

'Three! Hugo, Lucas and Theo and they're all older than me!'

I was curious. Were they male versions of Bee – pale-faced geeks or nerds with braces who recognized alliteration in everyday conversation? Or were they bronzed and buff, as the skateboards, skis and camping trip seemed to suggest? I couldn't wait to meet them.

'Is Ebyan coming?' said Bee, changing the subject.

'She's in the shop, remember?' said Keisha. 'But Mrs Warsame did say she can finish early.'

'That's something,' I said.

'If they're not too busy, like,' added Keisha.

'That's the end of that, then,' I said. 'They're always busy.'

'I'll get us some snacks,' said Bee. 'We've got pomegranate juice and *Maman* baked *madeleines.*'

We listened to her pounding back down the stairs and Keisha shrugged her shoulders and rolled her eyes.

'Pommie granite! Mad Ellen? I don't know how we got into this, like.'

'It was your idea,' I said. I switched on Bee's CD player and plugged my MP3 into the line-out port so we could all listen to my new Aaron B download. 'You were the one passing us off as image consultants.'

'Yeah, but you were the one saying all she needed was a makeover.'

I laughed and pointed to the king-size make-up bag I'd dumped on Bee's bed. It was stuffed full of skin-care products, make-up and various sponges and brushes.

'Well, if we can't sort her out with that lot, there's no hope.'

'Isn't that Aunty Dionne's?' said Keisha, nodding at the make-up bag as she emptied the contents of her own bag onto the bed – curling tongs, straighteners and loads of bottles of nail polish.

'She'll never miss it,' I said. 'Ever since Mum turned her back on modelling, she thinks make-up is the work of the devil. Anyway, it's mainly samples and freebies from cosmetics companies that still think models have to be pale and interesting instead of dark and lovely like us. They want her to do reviews or give endorsements but she doesn't even bother to open them.'

Bee came back, balancing an overloaded tray – and turned the music down a notch. Mrs Buchet's baking was a whole lot better than her hospitality. *Madeleines* turned out to be little shell-shaped cakes that tasted of oranges and I ate quite a few, washed down with the juice, before I set to work on Bee's face. I started with cleanser, toner and moisturizer.

'You've got great hair and skin,' I told her. 'No nits or zits.'

'I'm too pale,' said Bee. 'And I have too many freckles. *Maman* bought me some concealer to cover them up.'

'You shouldn't do that,' I said as I dusted a pale pink blush powder with glitter onto her cheeks and applied cream shadow above and below her eyes. 'Freckles are cute.'

I ignored the horrified expression that crept across

her face when she clocked the bright turquoise eye shadow, and I added heaps of black mascara which, in my not-so-humble opinion, looked brilliant. I finished the look with a swipe of red dazzle lip gloss.

'It's a bit intense for a Saturday afternoon,' said Keisha as she tilted Bee's chin and inspected my handiwork. 'But it would be good for a special occasion, like.'

Bee swivelled round and examined her reflection in the mirror.

'What? You mean like *Cirque du Soleil*?' she said. It was the nearest I had ever heard her come to a joke. 'I look like I'm wearing clown make-up!'

I grudgingly handed her an eye make-up remover pad and watched in alarm as she smudged the mascara into an inky black mess. She rubbed hard till her eyes were red and puffy and she looked like she had come off worst in a scuff with Bella Blake.

'Can you try something lighter?' said Bee. 'You know, *au naturel*. That's what I'll need for the Bright Sparks thing.'

She was right, of course, but her pale skin was now pink and blotchy and she wouldn't let me use foundation or bronzer to disguise it. I dabbed a touch of greyish-green on her eyelids and brushed light cherry sunburst sheen on her lips, but it was no substitute for serious camouflage.

'Sorry, Bee,' I said. 'Why don't we take a break?'

I munched another cake while Keisha started on Bee's hair. She twisted and teased it into tight ringlets with the curling tongs. She flattened the roots and ends with the straighteners, to stretch out the waves. Under the gentle rhythm of the finishing brush strokes, Bee closed her eyes and zoned out. Keisha clipped a small green feather fascinator above her ear.

'What do you think?' she whispered to me. 'I think she looks fabtastic.'

I agreed, but I wasn't sure about the fierce, fake claws she glued onto Bee's nails, especially when she painted them with a high-gloss jazzy jade.

After the first disaster, Bee was nervous about letting me anywhere near her face again. But after a bit of persuasion, I helped her find her inner beach babe with a sheer foundation and a dusting of coral powder on her nose, cheeks, lips and eyelids. I layered a warm, peachy blush over her cheeks, applied emerald liquid liner on her lower lids and added lots of clear lip gloss. The results were stunning, even if I do say so myself.

'Now for clothes, shoes and accessories,' said Keisha. 'I don't think Ebyan is going to make it, but I suppose we'll manage without her, like.'

She leaped up and threw open Bee's wardrobe and we gazed in stunned silence at the colour-coordinated outfits hanging from the rail and folded neatly on the shelves. The only problem was that half of it was navy-blue school uniform and the other half was navy-blue sportswear. There was lots of Lycra and Cool-Max polyester. I could guess what Keisha was thinking, but she refused to give up and started to rummage.

I realized that Bee was a bit of an action-girl. I had a sudden flashback of myself playing football in primary school and I felt a flurry of envy as I recalled our last high school achievement assembly.

'Didn't you win some kind of athletics trophy recently?' I said.

'I've actually won quite a few, especially outside school,' said Bee. She grinned shyly. 'Last year I set a new under-thirteen county record for the eight hundred metres. *Maman* has all my medals and trophies lined up with my brothers' stuff in a display cabinet downstairs.'

I would have liked to ask more – about the trophies *and* the brothers – but Keisha's head popped back out of the wardrobe. She had chosen blue jeans – what else? – plus a white T-shirt and silver flip-flops.

Bee is tall and leggy, which probably makes her a good athlete, but she is all gangly and knobbly-kneed. She is definitely no model. On top of that, the T-shirt was baggy and out of shape, the jeans were too short and the flip-flops were at least one size too small. But Keisha worked miracles. She tied a knot at one side of the T-shirt, rolled up the legs of the jeans, and hacked and frayed a few designer-style rips with her nail file and scissors. Tropical Bee was ready for her close-up.

That was the exact moment Bee's mother poked her head round the door. Her beady blue eyes scanned the room and she took in the mess of clothes and cosmetics scattered everywhere. I turned off the music and got ready to gather up Mum's stuff before Mrs Buchet booted us out onto the street. She looked hard at Bee. She blinked and her mouth moved, but for a moment or two no words came out.

'Béatrice!' she said at last. 'You look like a real . . . you look *très belle*! Beautiful.'

It could have gone either way and I heard myself gasp with relief.

'Well done, girls,' said Mrs Buchet. She looked from Keisha to me and actually managed a genuine smile. 'I have to admit, I had my doubts but you've done a great job.' She beamed at her daughter again. 'Come down to the garden. We have to take photos. It's marvellous to see you looking like a girl for a change instead of one of the boys. *Absolument fabuleux!*'

Mrs Buchet had a prehistoric monster of a digital camera and she took loads of pictures of all of us, in masses of different poses. We stretched out on the sun lounger and strutted our stuff along the garden wall. Bee slam-dunked a few basketballs, Keisha pirouetted across the patio and I dribbled a football across the lawn. When the camera battery went flat, Mrs Buchet transferred the images to her prehistoric monster of a computer and made me and Keisha a copy on CD, while the three of us drank the last of the pomegranate juice and I ate the last cake.

It was late afternoon when we left, and Keisha wanted to go to Suuqa Samiira to see Ebyan before the shop closed. Normally I would have gone with her but I gave her a quick hug and said goodbye. I couldn't wait to get home and log on to my own computer. I could hardly believe my luck. I hadn't had a clue how I was going to get a decent photograph of myself to send off for the first stage of the Bright Sparks competition. I'd been thinking of asking Bee to take one on her snazzy e-phone – but now I suddenly had loads of pictures to choose from.

I spent ages gazing at the action shots. I looked ridiculous playing football in a sundress and red canvas pumps but I remembered when I used to play for the Halsall under-twelves. Back then, I never used to give a second thought to what I looked like. As long as I had studded boots on my feet, I didn't care if I was wearing tatty tracksuit bottoms or scruffy shorts. I was one of only three girls in the whole team and all we had to do to impress the lads was score as many goals as they did.

I sighed. Girls were much more complicated. They could be all cool and ready to share their secrets one second, then switch and be completely vicious and ready to tear you to shreds the next. I used to prefer a kick-about with the lads because it was easier to deal with bruised shins than battered feelings.

But things changed when we left primary school. The boys suddenly became interested in girls in a different way and they didn't want to let me play – well, not football anyway. And to make things worse, most of them were loads better at making friends with girls than I was. It was pure luck that me and Keisha ended up at the same high school. At first, she'd wanted to go to some posh dance academy – and I was secretly glad that Aunty Esme and Uncle Devon hadn't been able to afford it. If I hadn't been moved to the same class as Keisha and Ebyan, I'd still be a Bella no-mates.

In the end, I chose a picture where I was perched on the garden wall, dangling my legs and not doing much at all. But I was wearing a cute smile, and in the sunlight my brown skin glowed and my eyes shone like new pennies. Against the clouds and pale blue sky, my hair was a halo of brown, sun-kissed curls.

I filled in the Bright Sparks registration form with my contact details, my interests and ambitions, my dress and shoe size – and my showcase talent, which obviously was playing the cello. At the bottom of the form, there was a statement about Internet safety. It said no photos or information would appear on the website unless contestants made it to the semi-finals – and would never include contact details. All the same, I still felt a flicker of panic as I uploaded my photo and pressed *send*. I knew Mum would go ballistic if she ever found out I was posting stuff online.

I heard a click from my inbox. I had received an instant automated reply. The office was closed until Monday. All I could do now was cross my fingers and toes – and wait.

# 3

## School

At school on Monday morning, Bella Blake was true to her word and started on her mission to make my life a misery. I hadn't even made it to our form room when I met her sauntering up the corridor in the opposite direction. She was with Madison and another girl called Ashleigh. Unfortunately, I was alone and I wondered if they'd been waiting to jump me.

'Look, it's little Miss Perfect,' said Bella as soon as she spotted me.

She barged my shoulder as I tried to walk past, so my ignore-her-and-keep-walking strategy fell apart immediately. I whirled round to confront her.

'What *is* your problem?'

Bella stepped in close and hissed into my ear, 'I don't have a problem. You do – and it's me!'

'Ooh,' I said, trying to play it cool. 'I'm so scared.'

'Scared?' said Bella. 'If that was what I wanted, I would have slapped you up and knocked you down already.'

'So what *do* you want?'

'That's for me to know and you to find out,' she said.

She whispered something to Madison and Ashleigh and they cackled with laughter. The bell went and the three of them melted into the crowd of other kids who were on their way to registration. Now I *was* scared. Bella was twice the size of me and she could have battered me any time she felt like it. She didn't want to jack my phone or my lunch money – that wasn't her style. So what was she up to?

I got an idea at break time. I was standing in the playground with Keisha, Ebyan and Bee, catching up on what had happened over the rest of the weekend, when I noticed the Bella Blake bullies giggling and whispering, and shooting dirty looks in our direction. I marched over.

'If you've got something to say, why don't you just tell me to my face?'

'Get a life,' said Ashleigh. 'Don't flatter yourself.'

'You're being paranoid,' said Madison. 'We weren't talking about you.'

'And even if we were, that's kind of the point,' said Bella. 'We'd have been talking *about* you, not *to* you.'

I decided to go back to Plan A and ignore them, but as I walked away I could hear Bella chanting a stupid rhyme behind me.

'*Little Miss Perfect, little Miss Pretty, little Miss Popular, Miss Little Titty.*'

I felt a hot rush of blood to my face as her mates fell about laughing. What a cow! Even if I was pretty, it could never make up for being completely flat-chested.

'Why didn't you back me up?' I snapped when I got back to my own friends.

'Do not let her get to you,' said Ebyan. 'Just keep out of her way.'

'She's, like, so not worth the trouble,' said Keisha.

'And you told me yourself,' said Bee. 'She's all bluff and bluster.'

I couldn't believe it! Bella Blake had already managed to turn my best friends against me. I could practically feel the knife stabbing me in the back!

I kept a low profile for the rest of the day and nothing much happened until last lesson, which was ICT. Ms Hacker rambled on about data validation and verification. It was as dry as dust. She was the worst teacher in the universe. She knew her stuff when it came to cyberspace, but she didn't have a clue about real life or real people.

She scrawled notes on the electronic white board, and when I got fed up with watching the machine transform her scribble into Times New Roman, I decided to check my email and see if there was anything from Bright Sparks. I logged on to my Firebrand account and scanned my inbox. Two people I didn't know wanted me to be their friend on Facebook, someone else wanted me to follow them on Twitter and there was a phishing scam about my non-existent bank account – and an email from Bright Sparks!

Re: BRIGHT SPARKS
From: Lucia Torino (lucia@brightsparks.co.uk)
Sent: Mon 11 June 09:13:01
To: Destiny Buckley-Reid (destiny@firebrand.co.uk)

Hi Destiny
We are pleased to tell you that you have been successful in reaching the second round of BRIGHT SPARKS and you are invited to attend a PHOTOSHOOT at 5pm on Thursday 14 June at:

FLORIAN BARTHOLOMEW PHOTOGRAPHIC STUDIO
MIDDLE TEMPLE STREET
BIRMINGHAM
B2 3HU

On arrival, there were will be a consultation with our photographer and assistant who will talk to you about how you would like to look in your finished images. Our make-up artist and hairdresser will then work their magic and transform the way you look.

We have a large range of designer and brand-name clothing, shoes and accessories and our stylist will assist you in choosing the best combinations to suit your unique style and personality and enable you to shine!

While the shoot is taking place, your family or friends can relax in our reception lounge.

When the shoot is finished, our experts will advise you on the best images to select for the website and give you the best chance of reaching the shortlist and showcasing your brains and talents at the final of BRIGHT SPARKS.

Please reply via the link below to confirm you will be attending your appointment and that you have read our
TERMS AND CONDITIONS:

http://www.brightsparks.co.uk

We look forward to seeing you soon and wish you the best of luck!

Lucia Torino

I just about managed to stop myself bouncing up from my chair and announcing my good news to the whole room. Instead, I reached across to the next computer station and poked Keisha in the ribs with my ruler to attract her attention. She was totally engrossed in the fascinating details of data entry and she squealed and leaped up off her seat. Before I knew it, Ms Hacker was leaning over my shoulder and blowing stale, stinky cigarette breath down my neck.

'Destiny Buckley-Reid!' she croaked. 'Just as I was beginning to think you might actually be more than just a pretty face. What on earth are you doing?'

I quickly clicked the log-out icon and didn't answer. Ms Hacker's glasses were dangling from the chain round her neck and not perched on the end of her pointy nose. With any luck, she hadn't been able to read the details of my email even though she must have seen exactly what I was doing. She cleared her throat, braying like a dying donkey, straightened up and spoke to the whole class.

'You are all aware that using school computers to access private email and unauthorized websites is strictly forbidden and any breaches of the rules will not be tolerated and will be severely punished.'

I shivered. The way she was banging on, I was beginning to think she would take me outside, slam me up against a wall – and shoot me!

'Report to my office at three-thirty,' she said, peering down her nose at me. 'I will be writing a letter for you to take home to your parents to inform them that you have been given an hour's after-school detention.'

Her rubber-soled sandals squeaked against the floor and put my teeth on edge as she returned to the front of the room and continued to drone on. I popped a Mini-Mint. I still wasn't listening. I was stressing. If Mum found out I had emailed Bright Sparks, I'd be grounded till I was forty. And if Bella Blake wanted to carry on tormenting me after school, now she would know exactly where to find me.

Ms Hacker kept me hanging around outside her office for ages. I listened to Aaron B on my MP3 and tried to imagine what it would be like to kiss Joel Daley-Clarke. But by the time Hacker handed me the letter, I felt as if I'd done half a detention already. Still, at least I was sure Bella would have gone home. She wouldn't have the patience to wait around to ambush me for that long. I opened the envelope as soon as I'd cleared the school gates and quickly ran my eyes down the page. There was no mention of Bright Sparks – just the stuff about personal email and unauthorized sites, plus a reminder of the home – school agreement, which all parents and students had to sign at the beginning of each school year. I stared at the last sentence, written in Hacker's usual scrawl: *Destiny has therefore been given an hour-long after-school detention on Thursday 14 June.*

Biff! Bam! Boom! Kill me now! Ms Hacker's detention was the same day as the Bright Sparks photoshoot!

When I got home, Dad was there – back from his tour of hotels in France and Spain. He's the General Manager so he's always off on some business trip or another – and I always miss him.

'Hello, beautiful, how's it going?' He threw his arms round me and hugged me tight to his chest.

'Hi, Dad,' I gasped, struggling to breathe. 'I'm fine. How are you?'

'Much better for seeing you,' said Dad, finally releasing me and letting me come up for air.

'Is Mum in?'

'Corner shop,' said Dad. 'Milk.'

I pulled Ms Hacker's letter from my bag. 'She has to sign this.'

Dad scanned the letter and reached for the pen in his suit pocket. 'I know you're not going to make a habit of this,' he said as he winked at me and scribbled his signature, 'so let's just pretend it never happened.'

I hugged him again and ran upstairs to avoid Mum.

I knew it wasn't quite what Dad meant but it was a good idea. Detention? What detention? I had a photo-shoot to attend!

I checked myself in the mirror to make sure that nothing was going to stand in the way of me looking my best. My skin was zit-free, but I carefully dabbed at my face with a deep-cleansing facial wipe to make sure it stayed that way. I dusted my cheeks with ultra-glow bronzer, added a touch of copper eyeliner to my lower lids and a light golden shimmer gel to my lips. Not bad – even with the subtle, low-key colours and no mascara!

I popped a Mini-Mint and opened my email account again to re-read the Bright Sparks email. This time, I studied the small print.

## BRIGHT SPARKS

### TERMS AND CONDITIONS

1. All entrants must complete the online registration form and upload a recent photograph.
2. If you are lucky enough to be selected by our panel of distinguished judges (some of whom are industry professionals, including agents, talent scouts, actors, musicians, voice and acting coaches), you will be invited to attend a professional photoshoot at the Florian Bartholomew Photographic Studios in Birmingham.
3. You will receive six free 8 x 10 inch (20.3 x 25.5 cm) prints for your portfolio and have the opportunity to purchase further prints if you wish.
4. If you reach the semi-finals, your profile and photographs will be posted online and your friends and family and members of the public will be able to vote for you online or by text.
5. Voting will end at midnight on 14 July. Any votes placed after this time may be charged but will not be counted.

6. To vote for you, your supporters should text your first and last name to 73032 or phone 0901 438 2840 and enter your contestant number. All calls and texts cost 60p plus standard network charge. All voters must have the permission of the bill payer.

7. The top ten girls from the public vote and the top ten girls selected by our panel of judges will be invited to attend the live final at the International Convention Centre in Birmingham at the end of July. Finalists will be announced live online and notified by email.

8. All entries must be accompanied by a consent form and the £100 entry fee.

Please download and print the CONSENT FORM, ask your parent or guardian to sign it and post it back to us at:

BRIGHT SPARKS, PO Box 100, Birmingham, B1 5JB
Please remember to enclose £100 to cover the costs of competition entry, administration, make-up and photoshoot, plus six photographs.

I immediately realized I'd made a big mistake. I should have showed Dad the consent form instead of the detention slip. There was no way he would sign it now. And where in the world was I going to get my hands on £100?

# 4

## Money

I decided not to hold a grudge and I forgave my friends
for not sticking up for me the day before. To be honest,
they behaved like nothing had happened and I don't
think they even noticed. It was lunch time and we were
sitting on the thin strip of grass near the teachers' car
park, sharing the school canteen's idea of a takeaway
picnic, which was the latest attempt to force us to eat
more healthily. I explained my problem with the
consent form and entry fees.

'You must have hundreds of pounds by now,' said
Keisha. 'I have.'

I nearly choked on my wholemeal sandwich. 'How?'

'From Nan,' said Keisha. 'Every Christmas and birthday since we were babies – a new dress and a ten- or
twenty-dollar bill. Mum changes it into pounds and

pays it into my savings account, like. I guess Aunty Dionne does the same with yours.'

'She's never mentioned it,' I said.

'Ask her about it,' said Keisha, wiping crumbs from her chin and taking a swig of water.

'No way,' I said. 'I can't tell her I need funds for the Bright Sparks contest.' I looked at Bee. 'How are you paying *your* entry fee?'

'*Maman* sent a cheque with the consent form. The money wasn't an issue because the whole thing was her idea in the first place.'

'Lucky for some,' I said.

'Maybe,' said Bee. 'I wanted to demonstrate my eight hundred metres warm-up routine for the talent showcase, but she's pushing me to do something girly – like ribbon-twirling or cheerleading! She's desperate for me to do something else besides sport.'

'Mothers! This could be my big musical break but my mum can't see past the beauty bit of the competition,' I said gloomily. 'She thinks being boring and ugly is the only way to avoid being big-headed and arrogant or skinny and anorexic. And she reckons it's wrong to judge people on how they look physically.'

'In athletics, people are judged on physical stuff all the time,' said Bee. 'If I get to the Olympics and I win a gold medal because I'm fitter and stronger and can run eight hundred metres faster than anyone else in the world, I'll be a hero.' She paused – probably to picture herself crossing the finishing line first as well as to catch her breath. 'There's nothing wrong with people winning prizes for running fast or juggling or playing the cello – or for looking good.'

I grinned at her. I needed to take this girl home and introduce her to my mother!

'You'll get an MBE like Kelly Holmes and Ellie Simmonds,' I told her. 'We'll have to call you Dame Bee.'

'It's not the same,' said Keisha, bursting the bubble. 'In sport, like, you use a stopwatch or a tape measure to judge who's the best. But how do you judge beauty?'

'You are right,' said Ebyan. 'Different people and different cultures do not agree. Even in a contest like Bright Sparks, which is supposed to value talent and brains and personality, an ugly girl is not going to win. A fat girl is not going to win. A girl wearing a *jilbaab* is not going to win.'

I sighed. Maybe they had a point but I didn't want to argue about it. I turned the conversation back to how I was going to get hold of some cash. Their ideas became more and more ridiculous.

'Baby-sitting.'

'Dog-walking.'

'Car-boot sale.'

'Rob a bank.'

I pointed out the obvious, of course. I don't like babies, I'm scared of dogs – except for Keisha's pooch, Diesel – I don't have a car and I don't want to end up as a young offender in Oakhill or Rainsbrook!

'Is Aunty Dionne at work today?' said Keisha, just as I was in the middle of giving serious consideration to the idea of hauling my cello into town and busking outside New Street train station.

'What's that got to do with the price of chickens in Bulgaria?'

'If she's out of the house, like, we could look for your savings book together.'

I popped a Mini-Mint. I knew I could rely on Keisha to come up with something useful if I was patient and gave her enough time.

Mum's desk was an old-fashioned bureau with a fold-down front and lots of different-sized pigeonholes inside and drawers underneath. It was locked.

'Where does she keep the key?' said Keisha.

I shrugged and looked around the living room, hoping for a flash of inspiration. When I didn't get one, I wandered around, peering into the fruit bowl, shaking vases and shifting a few books around on the shelves. The key could have been anywhere.

Keisha disappeared into the kitchen and a minute later she returned, brandishing a small brass key. I was impressed.

'Where did you find it?' I said as she slipped it into the lock.

'On the key hook next to the back door,' she said.

It was so obvious, I don't know why I hadn't thought of it myself. It's where Mum and Dad keep all their keys – garden shed, garage, car, bike lock, suitcases, spares – which, of course, is really handy for any passing burglars. I watched Keisha as she opened the lid to reveal the red-leather desk-top and the rows of small shelves, tightly packed with random bits of paperwork. Even if it actually existed, I realized that finding my bank book could take ages.

We thumbed our way through insurance policies, household bills, payslips, invoices and receipts. As well as mine and Mum's passports, I even found all our birth certificates and medical cards – but no bank book. We started on the drawers and finally, tucked beneath a pile of building society and bank statements, we found a small blue and green booklet, printed with the words *N S & I Investment Account passbook*. The front cover wasn't quite as wide as the rest of the booklet and my name was printed sideways down the edge of the first page, together with my account number. I flicked through the pages and a plastic card fell out onto the floor. I picked it up and turned it over in my hand. I'd been to the bank with Mum often enough to know that I needed a pin number to go with the card.

'I bet you a karaoke duet with a singing grizzly bear it's your birthday, like,' said Keisha.

I stared at her and hoped that whatever madness was going on inside her head would eventually stop and she would come to her senses. She tapped the plastic card with her candyfloss gloss-painted fingernail.

'The pin number,' she explained. 'I bet it's your date of birth.'

I grinned at her. I was ready to bet a twirl round a dance floor with a waltzing walrus she was right. I skimmed the pages of the passbook – which showed deposits from the time I was born – until I came to the most recent just after my last birthday. Keisha looked over my shoulder and we were both speechless as we stared at the current balance. I was rich! OK, not quite a millionaire but I did have £537.94.

We had to dig about on the Internet to find out where my life savings were actually being held. *Nsandi* sounded like a place in Zimbabwe but it turned out to be the post office. There was a branch on the high street, less than ten minutes away, and it was open till five. I tucked the savings book into my jeans pocket and

Keisha locked up Mum's desk. We set off in a burst of enthusiasm, but on the way I began to worry.

'Chillax,' said Keisha. 'What could possibly go wrong?'

I popped a Mini-Mint and didn't bother to answer, but inside my head I had a growing list of possible problems. Did I need ID to take money out of my account? What if the pin number was wrong? Did I need to be over eighteen? Would the post office tell Mum? By the time we got there and waited in line, I knew exactly what Nan meant when she Skyped and talked about being as nervous as a long-tailed cat in a room full of rocking chairs! We shuffled forward and finally the electronic voice called me to the counter:

'Cashier number three, please.'

My hand shook and I could hardly breathe as I slid the card into the chip and pin machine and slid the savings book across the counter.

'I would like to t-t-take out a hundred pounds, please,' I stuttered.

'Are you sure?' said Keisha, over my shoulder. 'You should take out more, like, in case of emergencies or in case you need to buy anything else.'

The cashier tilted his head to one side and tutted loudly. 'There's a hundred pound limit,' he said flatly.

'That's fine,' I said quickly. 'That's all I need.'

The cashier tutted again. 'And would you like to make a direct credit to another account or would you like that as a crossed warrant or in cash?'

I glared at Keisha, but she just turned her bottom lip inside out and shrugged. I turned back to the cashier and caught him rolling his eyes.

'I er . . . I don't have another account,' I said lamely.

'OK,' he said. 'That's a start.'

'And I need to send it off to Bright . . . to er . . . someone.'

'Postal order!' said the cashier, relieved. 'Can I suggest you purchase a postal order for one hundred pounds?'

'Yes, please,' I said gratefully. 'Thank you.'

'OK,' said the cashier, nodding towards the bank card reader. 'Enter your pin number.'

I crossed the fingers of my left hand and nervously tapped my birthday digits into the machine with my right. There were no flashing lights or sirens and when no one rushed in to arrest me, I remembered to breathe again. The cashier fed my passbook into a machine, counted out a hundred pounds from one compartment of his cash drawer and moved it to another. He slid the book and postal order across the counter, under the glass security screen.

'That's ten pounds, please,' he said, as I reached out to take them.

My hand hovered above the counter and I stared at him. Why hadn't he mentioned the cost of the postal order before? Desperate now, I turned to look at Keisha, but she shook her head before I even asked. It was a stupid question anyway. It wasn't as if she'd have a spare tenner tucked inside her bra.

For the first time, I noticed the long queue that had formed behind us. It zigzagged up and down between the moveable posts and giant elastic bands and out through the door. The people waiting had probably started off quiet and patient but now they shuffled restlessly and one or two muttered threats under their breath. One looked like a bouncer or a boxer and he shook his fist at us. But then I spotted Mrs Hagley, our rickety next-door neighbour, who scowled at him and told him to behave. There was no way she would be able to leap in and protect us if it came to a fight, but she was trying to keep the peace and she was the only person between us and an angry mob.

'Keep your hair on! Don't get your knickers in a twist,' she told them loudly, but when she caught my eye she tapped a finger on her watch and shook her head. 'What's the matter, Destiny?' she shouted, just in case anyone in the queue or behind the counter didn't know my name and didn't already suspect me of being up to no good. 'Are you short of money, dear? I can help you out and get it back off your mother later. How much do you need?'

'Ten pounds,' I muttered, edging along our side of the red band, which was all that was keeping the bouncer at bay.

Mrs Hagley pressed a grubby, crumpled ten-pound note into my sweaty palm and I shuffled all the way back and handed it to the cashier. Then I grabbed my savings book and the postal order and kicked out – fast.

# 5

## Forgery

I didn't catch up with Keisha until we were halfway home. I had a terrible stitch, but we kept running until we were back in the front room.

'We're so dead!' said Keisha as she tried to catch her breath. 'Mrs Whatshername is, like, so going to blab to Aunty Dionne.'

I was thinking the exact same thing myself but I tried to be positive.

'Mrs Hagley,' I said, filling in the gaps. 'As long as I return her ten pounds before she sees Mum, it will be fine.'

Keisha didn't look convinced, but I couldn't get into it. I had too many other things to worry about.

'Come on,' I said. 'Mum will be home any minute.

I need to put the savings book back in her desk. Where's the key?'

Keisha patted herself down. It was a bit pointless as she was still wearing her school uniform and it didn't have any pockets.

'I don't have it,' she said. 'I've lost it! I mean, you must have taken it.'

I didn't have it either but I suddenly realized Keisha had left it in the lock! I opened the drawer and slipped the savings book back under the bank statements.

'OK, now all I need to do is sign the consent form.'

'Sign the consent form?' said Keisha, repeating my words like a parrot and staring at me hard like a meerkat. 'Sign the consent form?'

I nodded.

'We are so dead!' she said again. 'I only agreed to help you look for your savings book, like. You never said anything about forgery!'

I stopped listening. I popped a Mini-Mint, opened the top of the bureau, took out Mum's passport and opened it to the back page.

Keisha leaned over my shoulder and let out a shriek. I thought she was still imagining us being thrown into prison for racketeering and fraud but I was wrong.

'That's the worst passport picture I've ever seen,' she said. 'How can they make a model look so bad?'

'Former model,' I said, correcting her. But I wasn't looking at Mum's photograph. I was looking at her signature. It was smaller than usual. It had been shrunk to fit into a tiny space in the bottom right-hand corner of the passport. All I had to do was copy it – and somehow expand it. I ran upstairs to fetch the Bright Sparks consent form. I spread it out on the table next to the passport. I had a last, quick look at Mum's signature and I signed the form quickly with a bold flourish.

'Not bad,' said Keisha with an approving nod.

She handed me an envelope from one of the pigeon-holes and I copied the Bright Sparks address from the form. I stuffed the postal order and form into the envelope and slammed the desk lid shut with a bang. There was a moment of stillness and then Mum's voice rang out, chillingly close.

'What are you doing?'

I turned my head round slowly. Mum stood in the living-room doorway, arms folded, face grim.

'Pardon,' I said, stalling and trying to buy thinking time.

'Don't play games, Destiny,' said Mum. 'What are you doing rifling through my desk?'

'Nothing,' I said lamely.

'Sorry, Aunty Dionne,' said Keisha smoothly, coming to the rescue. She snatched the envelope from my hand

and waved it above her head, like a flag. My stomach lurched. 'I need to post this for Mum. We were looking for a stamp.'

Mum unfolded her arms and smiled while I dissolved into a puddle of pure relief. Mum reached into her handbag and took out her purse.

'What do you need, sweetheart? First or second class?'

'First, please,' said Keisha.

Mum handed her the stamp. 'Are you staying for dinner?'

'No thanks, Aunty Dionne,' said Keisha. She smiled angelically, like butter wouldn't melt in her mouth.

Sometimes, I think Mum wishes Keisha was her daughter instead of me. I'm sure she would gladly do a swap with Uncle Devon and Aunty Esme. Mind you, to be fair, Keisha has an older sister and two older brothers from another mother who live in London, and Uncle Devon often says he would happily swap the whole lot of them for a red Ferrari! Keisha told me she didn't think he was joking either. He's a transport engineer and he says he has to work hard to clothe and feed four kids and pay for extras like ballet and driving lessons, plus food and vet fees for Diesel. My mum and dad work hard too but they only have me to look after, so I guess that makes it easier.

After Keisha left, I went upstairs to have a quick shower. I knew I could rely on her to post my application on the way home but I had literally been sweating buckets – and not just from running home from the post office.

After dinner, I slipped out of the house and went round to Mrs Hagley's. It took her about five minutes to shuffle to the door – and another five to undo the security chain.

'Blow my buttons, Destiny!' she yelled, loud enough for the whole street to hear. 'You live right next door but I don't see you from one month to the next and then I see you twice in one day! Come on in then, bab. Don't just stand there looking pretty.'

'It's OK,' I said, holding out my hands that were overflowing with the loose change I'd raided from my old money box. 'I just brought back your ten pounds.'

'It's good to clear your feathers, Destiny, but you didn't need to do that, you daft ha'p'orth,' said Mrs Hagley. 'I'd already forgotten all about it.'

As usual, I didn't understand half of what Mrs Hagley said and I didn't believe the other half.

'It's true,' she insisted, as if reading my mind. 'I'd forget me head if it wasn't screwed on. Come on, come in and put the wood in the hole.'

I guessed she meant that I should close the door but I had no idea why she didn't just say that.

'I can't come in,' I said. 'Really. I've got loads of homework and cello practice to do.'

'You young 'uns are always in such a rush,' said Mrs Hagley. 'One o' these days you'll meet yourself coming back.'

I gave up. 'Just for a minute then,' I said.

She led me into her front room, which was stuffed full of ornaments and pictures and smelled musty, as always. I dropped the coins onto her coffee table.

'Would you like a cuppa?' she said, padding off to the kitchen without waiting for an answer.

I sighed and plonked myself down on her lumpy sofa. Now I was never going to get away.

'Well,' said Mrs Hagley, finally handing me a flowery cup and saucer. 'What were you up to this afternoon? Are you tryin' to pull a fast 'un?'

I groaned – but not out loud. Mrs Hagley might be ancient but, to use one of her own sayings, she wasn't as green as she was cabbage-looking.

'Good on you, girl,' said Mrs Hagley when I finished telling her all about Bright Sparks. 'I know I look like a bag of muck tied up ugly, but in my day I was a real smashing-looking stunner, like you. I used to make the lads sigh at their suppers.'

Mrs Hagley had dodgy hips, wrinkled papery skin and white fluffy hair. It was hard to imagine she'd ever been young – and harder still to imagine she'd been pretty.

'Don't you dare!' she warned, reading my mind again. 'It's rude to ask a lady her age. I'm as old as me tongue and a bit older than me teeth!'

She heaved herself up from her armchair and took down a framed photograph from the top of her display case and handed it to me.

'That's me and our Eric, that is,' she said. 'Look at him in his best bib and tucker and me all dressed up to the nines. He won my heart with a trip up town and a Knickerbocker Glory. Handsome, he was – like Nat King Cole – and that lucky he'd have fell off the top of Rackham's into a new suit.'

I gazed at the picture. Mrs Hagley really had been a smasher! She was wearing a fitted blouse, a narrow pencil skirt, high heels – and gloves! Eric was wearing a waistcoat, a bow tie and a hat. The image was faded and grainy but I could still see that he was black.

'What happened to him?' I said.

'He fell off the front step!'

I nearly dropped the photograph. Was she serious?

'It's true,' she said sadly, staring into space. 'He'd been out on the razzle, and when he came home he fell over and hit his head. They didn't scan him until it was too late and there was internal bleeding in his brain.'

I didn't know what to say.

'Any road up,' said Mrs Hagley, suddenly changing the subject. 'You'd better be off home and tell your mother about this beauty contest malarkey or you'll catch it when she finds out.'

She took back the photograph and returned it to the display cabinet. I stood up, still reeling and speechless, and followed her to the front door.

'Ta-ra a bit, Destiny,' yelled Mrs Hagley when we finally got there. 'It was good to see you, even if it was short and sweet like a roasted maggot!'

# 6

## Shoot

Maybe it was something to do with being the only girl with so many brothers, but I began to think Bee could wrap her mother round her little finger. Somehow, she had managed to persuade her mum to phone Bright Sparks and ask them to re-schedule her photoshoot for the same day and time as mine. It was a clever move – and everything was going well. If I turned up with Mrs Buchet, no one would start asking me awkward questions about why I hadn't brought along an adult. When I didn't arrive home from school at the usual time, I knew Dad would crack and tell Mum I had been given a detention. And if I was really late getting back, Keisha would cover for me if Mum started to worry and began ringing round to see where I was. Yippity, skippity! Thursday could not come fast enough!

When it finally did, I left school casually, together with Keisha, Ebyan and Bee so I didn't attract any attention. I don't know what I would have done if we'd bumped into Bella or Ms Hacker, but luckily we didn't. Bee and I said goodbye to the others on the high street and caught the bus into town to meet Mrs Buchet, who was waiting for us at the bus stop in Corporation Street. She'd driven into town earlier in the day to go shopping and have her hair done, and before we went to the studio she took us to Sweet Pea's for a burger and chips – veggie and low-fat, of course.

The Florian Bartholomew Photographic Studio was in a sparkling new building on Middle Temple Street, just the other side of the Plaza Shopping Centre, so it was easy to find and we arrived on the dot of five. The entrance had an enormous revolving glass door. Inside, the foyer was equally slick. There was a row of lifts with silver doors and a glass-panelled reception desk. A fat security guard was sitting behind the desk, reading the *Evening Mail*, but when he heard Mrs Buchet's heels click-clacking across the polished floor, he leaped up and beamed us a friendly smile.

'Good evening, ladies,' he said. 'Third floor. Go straight up.'

Bee pressed the lift call-button and the doors swished open. Moments later, we stepped out into the studio. It was like walking into a big, shiny white box. There were a few people milling about and a tall, skinny man glided towards us as if he was walking down a cat-walk. He flicked back his dark, floppy hair and shook our hands. He had large brown eyes with long black lashes which made him look like a giraffe.

'*Bonjour, bonjour,*' he gushed. '*Je suis le photographe. Je m'appelle Florian Bartholomew.*'

'*Bonjour, Monsieur Bartholomew,*' said Mrs Buchet.

'*Bonjour, Florian,*' said Bee.

'Darlings,' he said. 'Call me Flor.'

'Hello, Flor,' I said firmly, just to remind everyone I was there and that I've only been studying French for two years. 'I'm Destiny and this is Bee.'

'We are expecting you,' said Flor. 'We have received your consent form and your cheque, no? Then follow me.'

He steered Mrs Buchet in the direction of the lounge and told her to help herself to a *café au lait*. Then we followed him across the studio to where the make-up artist and hairdresser were waiting to get their hands on us. I felt a flurry of excitement as they set to work, although they had forgotten the promised chat about what kind of image we were going for. The hairdresser scraped my hair back into a tight, eye-watering pony-tail, added long, straight temporary extensions and draped them over my shoulder. With my curls gone, I hardly recognized myself. The make-up artist dusted my face with powder that was too light for my natural complexion and added violet eye shadow.

'Wow!' she said. 'That really makes your eyes pop!'

I shuddered. I think she meant it made my eyes look bigger, but actually they also looked a bit bloodshot. She curled my eyelashes and smudged dark brown eye-liner on my lower lids. She applied purple mascara and slapped on plum-coloured blush and a burgundy lip gloss. My eyes watered even more.

'No tears, sweetheart,' she warned. 'We don't want you to smudge and run. You look beautiful. Remember, make-up needs to be dramatic for a photoshoot.'

Next it was the stylist's turn. She already knew our sizes from the application forms. Dressing up was fun and I finally started to enjoy myself. We tried on a few outfits, and the stylist and I agreed I would start with a slinky, sunset-orange, fitted mini dress, decorated with clusters of tiny bronze beads. It was way too big, but it took her about five seconds flat to pull it in and pin it at the back so that it looked as if it fitted me perfectly. I felt really glamorous, especially when she added a bronze and copper crystal tiara to my hair.

Then it was time for the pictures. Flor and his assistant had already set up the equipment and he pulled funny faces at me to make me laugh and help me get rid of my nervousness. Trust me, modelling is not easy! OK, it's not like cleaning toilets or maths homework, but it was still exhausting. I was wearing orange peep-toed shoes with four-inch heels. Standing still wasn't too bad – but walking? No way!

My second outfit was a black cross-back vest with matching, full-length skinny sports pants and high-tops in a candy pink, green and yellow colour-block design. Much more me – and a lot more comfy. My third outfit was a pair of chocolate brown cropped trousers with a high, wide waistband, together with a white T-shirt and strappy, wedge-heeled sandals.

Bee's make-up was even more extreme than mine. She had long, deep blue, feathered eyelashes to match the turquoise rhinestones that were dotted along her cheekbones. With the stylist's help, she went for a wild triangle-print, slim-fit mini dress with a scooped neckline and long sleeves, teamed with flat, black patent leather ballerina pumps. Her second outfit was a classic black zip-through tracksuit with a white three-stripe detail on the sleeves and legs, together with white leather high-tops with yellow eyelets and laces. Her final choice was a pair of red and black leopard-print skinny jeans with zipped pockets, together with a black mesh top and snake-effect shoe-boots with a concealed platform and slim heels. Even from the lounge on the other side of the studio, Mrs Buchet's eyes nearly popped out of her head! I don't think Bee's image was what her mother thought of as girly.

When Flor showed us the shots on the computer screen, I was amazed at the difference between the actual studio setting and what appeared in the final photos. The blue-screen backgrounds had been transformed into local landmarks and attractions – Selfridges' giant sequin-covered blob in the Bullring, the haunted Aston Hall manor house, the domed glasshouses in the Edgbaston botanical gardens. It was easy to forget there had been a whole crew of people – someone adjusting lights and holding up a reflective screen and someone else holding a small wind machine. It was all pretend.

Another girl turned up for her photoshoot, so Flor hustled me and Bee across the studio and back behind the screens to remove our make-up and change back into our school uniforms. The girl was older than us and somewhere between us in height. She had long black hair and perfect skin. She wasn't wearing any make-up and she was dressed in combats and boots but she was totally beautiful without even trying. She noticed me staring at her.

'What are you gawping at?' she snarled. 'Do you want a photo?'

I turned away sharply. She wasn't so pretty after all! I popped a Mini-Mint and we finished changing in silence. I followed Bee back across the studio to where her mother was waiting in the lounge.

'I will post the best five or six pics on the website ready for the public vote,' called out Flor as we left. 'You should be able to see them by about nine o'clock tonight and your prints will be posted to you in the next couple of weeks.'

He blew fake kisses across the white space before turning his attention and his camera back to Miss Bitchy Boots.

I could see from the shocked expression on Bee's face that she was having second thoughts about the competition and we didn't say much in the car as Mrs Buchet drove us home.

Later, when I logged on to the website and stared at our photos, I had a few second thoughts of my own. Our clothes and make-up – and the poses – made us look older than we were, but it was still hard to see how either of us could win against someone like Miss Bitchy Boots. I wondered if she even had a special talent.

Next to the pictures, neon-pink text glowed against a cream background. Our first names, achievements and aspirations had been taken from our application forms – Bee's eight hundred metres county record and her plans for the Olympics, and even my ambition to be a musician and combine R & B and classical music. Miss Bitchy Boots wanted to travel, save the world and work with small children and furry animals. Yeah, right!

# 7

## Stroke

I didn't sleep well. The next morning, I woke up with a headache. I didn't know whether to keep Bright Sparks a secret at school or whether to try and drum up support. In the end, I didn't have the chance to decide. Something terrible happened to me.

It was the worst thing in the world. I was sitting next to Ebyan in history, thinking about how I could get enough online and text votes, when I first noticed that something was wrong.

The side of my mouth was swollen, as if one of Bella Blake's bullies had just sparked me. I wondered if I had bitten my lip – maybe at the same time as I'd eaten my toast for breakfast or maybe when I'd popped my last Mini-Mint.

I gently ran my index finger round the edge of my

lips. They were all fat and puffy and I noticed a slight tingling sensation. Perhaps I was getting a cold sore or a great big fat zit. Fabtastic! That was just what I needed to persuade everyone to use their time and their phone credit to vote for me – not.

After a while, the strange feeling in my lip crept across my face to my cheek. My skin crawled – literally – as if mini beasts and bugs were burrowing into my flesh. I shuddered.

I glanced around the classroom to see if anyone else had noticed what was happening to me. Keisha was sitting miles away and didn't even look in my direction. Joel Daley-Clarke smiled and winked at me, but for once that wasn't what made my heart beat out of my chest. I turned away quickly.

I felt as if I had pins and needles in the whole left side of my face. I ran both sides of my fingers across my cheek. My skin felt tingly and ultra-sensitive, but beneath it my flesh was frozen and lifeless. Dead.

I nudged Ebyan. She turned round and I tried desperately to signal my growing alarm, silently with my eyes. She nudged me back and grinned, oblivious to my terror. She didn't understand me the way Keisha did. My heart pounded louder and faster. I took a deep breath.

'My mouth feels all numb,' I whispered.

'Numb?' said Ebyan. 'What do you mean?'

'It feels like the side of my face has gone to sleep or like I've just come back from the dentist.'

'It looks all right,' said Ebyan, peering at me. 'It's probably just where you've been leaning your head on your hand.'

OK, propping up my head and resting my chin in the palm of my hand was my favourite thinking position – even if I had been dreaming about Bright Sparks instead of reflecting on the disadvantages of the Industrial Revolution – but I wasn't convinced.

'Maybe,' I said doubtfully.

'Destiny, please concentrate,' said Mr Khan. 'If you have something interesting and important to say, you can share it with everyone.'

I didn't want to say anything in front of the whole class, but I began to think I didn't have much choice. As I rolled my swollen tongue over my teeth and round the inside of my cheeks, a trickle of saliva escaped from the corner of my mouth and dribbled down my chin. I wiped it away with my sleeve. Mr Khan had already moved on to talk about children's working conditions in the iron foundries. I had to put my hand up and wave frantically to attract his attention.

'Yes, Destiny.' He sounded impatient. 'What is it?'

'I've got a weird taste in my mouth,' I said. 'Like metal.'

'Like iron, I suppose,' said Mr Khan. 'Are you trying to be funny?'

'Her face is numb too,' said Ebyan.

'Do you have braces?' said Mr Khan, suddenly deciding to take me seriously now Ebyan had spoken.

I shook my head.

'Any other bits of hardware in your mouth?' said Mr Khan, with a frown. 'Any studs or barbells or rings in your cheeks or lips or tongue?'

I shook my head again as a low-key murmur of surprise rumbled round the room.

'Many ancient civilizations had tattoos and piercings,' said Mr Khan by way of explanation. 'The Mayans, Incas, Aztecs, Polynesians, Greeks, Egyptians, Nubians, Gauls – and more recently, the Brits.'

I briefly wondered if Mr Khan would tell that to Mum. I'd been bugging her about getting a tiny tribal-style Aquarius tattoo on the back of my neck, but the way she was over-reacting, anyone would think I wanted fifty stars and thirteen stripes on my face. Then I noticed that Mr Khan was eyeballing me as if I was already plastered in tattoos. Or maybe he'd suddenly noticed what I'd always heard from others – that I was actually quite pretty. Yeah, right. Even if it was true, he would probably describe me as comely or winsome because he wouldn't want to miss a chance to extend our vocabulary and increase our cross-curricular learning.

'You do look a bit sallow and poorly,' he said. 'It's almost break time, Destiny. Why don't you go and get some fresh air and a glass of water? If you don't feel better by the start of next lesson, come and see me in the staff room.'

Sallow? Poorly? I gathered my books and pencil case together and stuffed them in my bag. I didn't feel that bad, but I wasn't about to turn down the chance of getting out of history ten minutes early and escaping from Mr Khan's insults.

'Ebyan,' said Mr Khan. 'Can you please go with her?'

I had a bottle of water and a Bizarre Bar in my bag so we went straight out to the playground and sat on a bench.

'Do you want a piece?' I asked Ebyan.

'No thank you,' she said. 'That is probably why you feel sick.'

'I haven't eaten it yet,' I said, taking a big bite. 'And I don't feel sick.'

'Yes,' said Ebyan. 'But I still think that the worry and stress of hiding Bright Sparks from your parents combined with a sugar rush and crash—'

I didn't hear the rest of Ebyan's theory because I suddenly leaped up and spat out a half-chewed mouthful of biscuit and caramel. It tasted disgusting! I popped a Mini-Mint and took a big swig of water to take away the taste of the Bizarre Bar, but most of it dribbled down my chin and onto my blazer. Ebyan stared at me like I had grown an extra head.

'Sit down!' she snapped. She looked terrified.

I was so surprised, I immediately did as I was told.

'Stay there!' she ordered. 'I am going to fetch Mr Khan. Don't move.'

Ebyan hitched up her skirt and raced across the playground. I was stunned. She never ran anywhere except across a basketball or tennis court when Ms West absolutely insisted. I rubbed my palm against the side of my face. My cheek was still numb and now my left eye would not close properly. What was wrong with me?

The bell rang for break time and the playground flooded with kids. Keisha and Bee rushed over to join me on the bench.

'Cuz!' said Keisha. She eyed me nervously. 'What happened?'

I was still gobsmacked and couldn't speak. Bella and her crew of twisted sisters draped themselves across the bench opposite and were soon up to their usual tricks. They stared and pointed and whispered amongst themselves. What I couldn't understand was that half the school seemed to have flash-mobbed me! And they were all staring and whispering too. Mr Khan's voice rang out across the playground.

'Move along! Show's over! There's nothing to see here.'

He carved a path through the crowd and strode towards me, with Ebyan still running to keep up with him. When he reached my bench, he took one look at me and turned back towards Ebyan.

'Go and see Mrs Obodo,' he began. But we could all see how much Ebyan was huffing and puffing, after running backwards and forwards across the playground and up and down two flights of stairs. 'No! Beatrice, you go,' he ordered. 'Tell her to call an ambulance. Tell her it's urgent. Tell her it's an emergency.'

Now I was really scared! I watched Bee take off across the playground as if her Olympic gold medal depended on it.

'W-what is it?' I said frantically, looking up at Mr Khan. 'What's the matter?'

My left eye wasn't working at all now and my words sounded garbled and strange. Something horrible and horrendous was happening to me.

Mr Khan whirled round to face the cluster of kids who were still milling around.

'Break is over!' he roared. 'Back to class right now!'

'Not me,' said Ebyan, still panting for breath. 'I am not leaving her.'

'Nor me,' said Keisha. 'If she has to go to hospital, like, I'm going with her.'

'P-please. S-s-stop. I don't need to go to hospital,' I said, still slurring my words. 'I just . . . I just need to go home and lie down.'

Mr Khan didn't bother to argue with any of us. He lowered himself onto the bench beside me, muttering under his breath.

'Fast,' he murmured, looking hard at my face. 'Yes, that's it. F for face. Can you smile, Destiny?'

I stared back at him, bewildered. I tried to smile but even without being able to see myself, I could tell it wasn't quite working. My smile felt lop-sided and crooked.

'A for arms,' muttered Mr Khan. 'Can you lift up your arms?'

He was alarming me but I did what he asked. At least my body was working all right.

'S for speech, T for time,' said Mr Khan. He leaped up from the bench. 'Time! Time! Where is the blasted ambulance?'

As if he had summoned it himself, the blaring sound of a siren cut through the stunned silence that had descended over the playground. Moments later, two paramedics in green overalls jogged towards us. The small knot of stubborn kids still hanging around parted to let them through.

'Honestly,' I yelled desperately, 'I don't need to go to hospital.'

The paramedics ignored me. They gave me an aspirin, strapped me to a stretcher and slapped an oxygen mask over my face so I couldn't speak any more. They wheeled me to the ambulance and slid me in through the back doors. The flashing blue light shone through tinted window in the roof and bounced off the machines and instruments. Mrs Obodo waddled up the steps and sat in the passenger seat at the foot of the stretcher. Just before the paramedics slammed the doors and turned the siren back on, I heard the last snatch of conversation from the playground.

'Why can't I go with her?' said Keisha. 'What's the matter with her?'

'She has to be accompanied by a responsible adult,' said Mr Khan. 'I think she's had a stroke!'

The ambulance was cold. As we bounced over potholes in the side roads, all I could think about was Mr Khan's last words. A stroke? Was I going to die? Stupid, stupid question. Of course, I was! I'd had a stroke! But I didn't want to. I wasn't ready. I had so much to live for. Too much to do. My friends and family would miss me. I lifted the oxygen mask away from my face and looked at the paramedic.

'Tell my mum and dad that I love them,' I whispered croakily.

'You can tell them yourself,' he replied. 'They're meeting you at the hospital.'

They're trained to say stuff like that. They don't just tell someone straight out that they're not going to make it – even if, like me, they can hardly catch their breath and there's a pounding pain behind their eyes that feels about a hundred times worse than biting into an ice cream. Even if they actually die, like Nan's boyfriend.

A stroke? No way! I didn't believe it. I wouldn't believe it!

When we reached what must have been the Aston Expressway the driver put his foot down. It was a fast and bumpy ride and Mrs Obodo spent the whole journey with her eyes squeezed closed, gripping the edge of her seat. She was no use at all.

Before long we arrived at Birmingham Children's Hospital – because there isn't one for teenagers. Half of the building was like a Victorian castle and the other half looked like it was built out of Lego. I caught a quick glimpse of the flashy glass canopy over the main entrance before I was whisked round the corner to another entrance, where I saw the Accident and Emergency sign. I was flat out on a trolley, and as I was wheeled down an old-fashioned corridor, I gazed upwards to where weak sunlight filtered through high-panelled windows and cast long, grey shadows of the paramedics across the walls. I felt as if I'd been abducted by aliens for scientific investigation and experimentation.

In the treatment room, Martians disguised as nurses took my temperature, pulse and blood pressure. They put a needle in the back of my hand and threaded a plastic tube into a vein and sucked out my blood. A Venusian disguised as a doctor hooked me up to an ECG machine to check my heart and a Jupiterian wheeled me away for X-rays.

Even without all the poking and prodding, I could have told them that things weren't going well. The whole left side of my face felt crumpled and numb. My eye was twitching and watering, but it still felt dry. My mouth was droopy and lopsided. My speech was even more slurred. I dribbled uncontrollably. There was an annoying buzzing noise in my ear – although that might have just been the aliens when they started interrogating me.

'Do you have epilepsy?'

'Do you suffer from migraines?'

'Do you have any allergies?'

'Have you taken any drugs?'

'No!' shrieked a high-pitched voice I would have recognized from outer space.

Whoop! Whoop! Mum had come to rescue me! OK, she didn't immediately smuggle me out of the bed and into a getaway car, but she did send Mrs Obodo back to school. She made everyone else introduce themselves properly and stop asking me daft questions. And she made them answer a few questions of my own.

'What exactly is a stroke?' I whispered, squashing down my fears and plucking up the courage to ask.

Stroke. It sounded so gentle. It was what Keisha did to Diesel's back, in between rubbing his belly and scratching behind his ears. But I already knew it wasn't that kind of stroke. It was the sort that had killed Nan's boyfriend – the nearest Keisha and I had to a grandfather!

'A stroke is what happens when a blood vessel in the brain gets clogged or bursts,' said one of the A & E aliens. I think her name was Dr James. 'It paralyses people on one side of the body.'

I shuddered and shook as I swallowed down a

scream. I wished I hadn't asked. But I was on a roll and I couldn't stop myself. I asked about all the tests and treatments – and finally, I asked the most important question of all.

# 8

## Casualty

*Am I going to die?*

I was admitted to the Observation Unit so I could be monitored overnight in case I got worse. The walls were painted in bright primary colours, which might have helped distract a six-year-old from all the tubes and wires but were doing nothing for me.

*Am I going to die?*

A few hours later, my whole family had gathered round my bed. My eye was still watering, but I managed to squint around at everyone. Dad's white, rosy-cheeked face was now grey and grim. Mum's eyes were ringed with red and her brown cheeks were stained white with dried tears. Aunty Esme's forehead was folded into worried ripples and the corners of Uncle Devon's mouth drooped into his goatee. Keisha's bottom lip wobbled uncontrollably. There were notices up all over the place that said patients were only allowed two visitors at a time. I was already up to five and none of the nurses said anything. It was a sure sign that my health was going rapidly downhill.

*Am I going to die?*

It didn't matter how many times I asked, no one would answer me.

'You look exhausted,' said Mum. 'I'll stay, but maybe everyone else should leave you to get an early night and see how you are in the morning, after a sleep.'

An early night is Mum's answer to everything. If I get a cold, she smears my back and feet with Vicks and tells me to go to bed. If I get period pains, she fills me a hot-water bottle and tells me to go to bed. If she's really worried, like today, she phones Aunty Esme – and I still end up in bed! Aunty Esme is a nurse. Well, a community midwife, to be exact, but she couldn't fob me off like everyone else.

*Am I going to die?*

'You'll be fine,' said Aunty Esme quietly, struggling to keep the cracks out of her voice.

Keisha burst into tears. 'How do you know?' she sobbed. 'Look what happened to Grandad!'

Aunty Esme glared at her daughter. 'Listen, honey,' she said, turning and looking at me. 'Grandad was old.

You are fit and young. Lots of people recover from strokes and . . .'

'Let's not get ahead of ourselves,' warned Dr James. 'Let's wait till tomorrow when Destiny has been seen by a specialist and had a few more tests.'

'Who?' snapped Dad. He sounded really bad-tempered but it was just the stress. 'What?'

'Doctor Gopalaswarmi,' said Dr James. 'He's the specialist consultant paediatric neurologist.'

'And what exactly will Doctor Gopalaswarmi do?' demanded Dad.

'He will decide whether Destiny should have a CT or an MRI scan,' said Dr James. 'He will make the final diagnosis.'

*Am I going to die?*

The next day was Saturday. I'd hardly slept and it was still early o'clock when I spotted Dr James and another doctor whispering near the nurses' station. Dr James had bed hair and big bags under her eyes. She looked like she hadn't slept much either. The other doctor looked like he was dressed for a game of cricket instead of giving a second opinion on my life expectancy. He wore a creamy chunky-knit sleeveless jumper and baggy white trousers.

'Must be the specialist consultant paediatric

neurologist,' whispered Mum as she yawned and stretched, and stood up from the armchair at the side of my bed where she'd spent the night.

'The very one!' said the doctor loudly.

I stared at him. He must have better hearing than Diesel! He strode towards us across the Observation Unit together with Dr James. The only thing that made him look like a doctor was the badge pinned to his jumper that read *Dr Sundeep Gopalaswarmi*. There was a long list of letters after his name.

'You can call me Doctor Sunny,' he said, when he noticed me reading the tag.

He scrunched up his eyes and squinted at me through his wire-rimmed glasses for all of about ten seconds before turning back to the A & E doctor.

'We don't need to bother with any more tests, Doctor James. Please cancel the scan and arrange for Miss Buckley-Reid to be discharged from the Observation Unit.'

Mum, Dr James and I gaped at him in astonishment. What did he mean? Was there no hope for me at all? Dr Sunny removed his glasses. He took a handkerchief out of his trouser pocket and polished them.

'Don't worry, Destiny,' he said. 'I have good news . . . and better news.' He put his glasses back on, touched a finger to his fat black moustache and grinned at what he clearly thought was a clever little joke. 'You have not had a stroke.'

'So what is it?' demanded Mum and Dr James in unison.

'Bell's Palsy,' said Dr Sunny, still looking at me.

My heart missed a beat. Bell's whatsy?

'There's a problem with one of the nerves in your face,' continued Dr Sunny. 'It's a little scary, I know, but it's nowhere near as serious as a stroke and definitely not life-threatening. Your face is paralysed, but I promise it won't last long and it will go away without any treatment.'

A little scary? What was he on about? I was still mega-terrified!

'We used to treat Bell's Palsy with anti-virals and steroids,' said Dr Sunny. 'But that's old hat now. I'll prescribe eye-drops to stop your eye drying out and patches to stop it being damaged and we'll see you again in a week or two.'

Still we stared.

'Is that it?' said Mum, echoing my thoughts. 'Isn't there anything else you can do?'

'No need, truly,' said Dr Sunny. 'Trust me, I'm a doctor.' He beamed at us. 'It was good to meet you both and I'll see you again in the outpatients department in a couple of weeks to see how you're progressing.'

'He's probably rushing home to watch the cricket,' whispered Mum – but she waited until he had disappeared and the unit doors had stopped swinging so he wouldn't overhear her again.

Mum couldn't wait to get me out of there. She swung into action. She dashed around the unit, finding my clothes, ordering a nurse to remove the tube from my hand, signing the discharge form and collecting the prescription. She phoned for a taxi even before she phoned Dad to tell him we were on the way home. She pushed me to the hospital exit in a wheelchair. Out of my good eye – the one that wasn't leaking water and covered with an eye-patch – I caught a fleeting glimpse of myself in the door of a stainless-steel medicine cabinet being wheeled in the opposite direction. It was hard to tell whether the mangled face that glanced back was really me – or whether it was distorted by speed and shock or by the scratched and dented surface of the metal. Either way, it didn't look great.

At home, Dad had brought my duvet and pillows downstairs and he tried to bundle me onto the sofa. He had loaded the coffee table with magazines, the remote controls for the TV and music system and a year's supply of my favourite drinks and snacks. I knew what he was up to. He didn't want me to go upstairs –

because that's where all the mirrors are. But unless Mum and Dad were prepared to fight me or tie me down, there was nothing they could do to stop me.

I heard Mum suck in her breath as I climbed the stairs, and when I turned round, her face crumpled as the tears started to fall.

'Come on,' said Dad. He slipped his arm round her shoulders and guided her towards the kitchen. 'I'll make you a cup of tea.'

I sucked in a big breath of my own. I went into the bathroom and bolted the door behind me. The mirror there was as good as anywhere else. Anyway, I needed to have a shower and clean my teeth because I hadn't had time to do it in the hospital. I leaned my back against the door, slid down and sat on the floor. I hugged my knees to stop them trembling. I desperately wanted to see exactly what I looked like now, but I had to prepare myself. I had to find the courage to look at the reflection of my ruined face. I tried to remember other times when I'd needed to be brave – diving in at the deep end of the swimming pool, playing a cello solo in the school concert, standing up to Bella Blake and saving Bee. It didn't help. They were all things with happy endings – and none of them had changed the way I looked and affected my whole life.

I wiped a bubble of spit from the corner of my

mouth with the back of my hand. I pushed the eye-patch up onto the top of my head, like one side of a pair of shades. Both my eyes were watering now, but with the heat and sting of real tears. My head throbbed and my heart thumped. I clenched my fists and forced myself to stand up – then, before I had time to change my mind, I looked in the mirror.

The glass was cracked!

I quickly turned away and looked back again. No, my face was cracked! I looked like I'd been whacked round the face with a frying pan!

I tried to squeeze my eyes shut but my left eye stayed open, still staring in disbelief at my reflection. When I raised my eyebrows, only the right-hand side of my face registered my horror. My left eye was half closed and droopy, my cheek was crumpled and sagged down-wards towards my chin and the side of my mouth was crooked and twisted!

I looked even worse than I'd imagined and the scream I'd choked down yesterday exploded in my chest and burst out of the side of my mouth. I threw up in the sink. My legs shook and gave way and I collapsed into a heap on the floor.

I vaguely heard the sound of someone hammering on the bathroom door, but it was almost drowned out by a terrible howling, wailing noise. It was some time before I realized it was coming from me. I sobbed into the bath mat, gulping in air and snorting out snot. I definitely wasn't pretty now. My face looked like a traffic accident.

I was ugly!

Who would like me now? No one would even look at me – except to point and stare.

# 9

## Home

I must have cried myself to sleep on the bath mat, because the next thing I knew the front doorbell was ringing and I heard voices from the hall.

'Hello, girls,' said Dad. His voice was croaky and anxious. 'It's good of you to drop by, but I don't think Destiny is up to having visitors.'

'Hello, Uncle Alan,' said Keisha.

'Hello, Mr Buckley-Reid.' I could just imagine Bee flashing her braces and giving him one of her best smiles.

'*Iskawaran*,' said Ebyan. She caught herself and switched effortlessly from Somali to English. 'Good afternoon, Mr Buckley-Reid. Please just give us five minutes and then we promise to leave.'

Silence. Dad was obviously thinking it over and I

willed him to say no in any language at all and send them away. But I heard Mum's voice call out from the front room.

'Let them in, Alan,' she said. 'If they can coax Destiny out of the bathroom, I can finally use the loo and maybe we can persuade her to eat something.'

I heard Keisha stomp up the stairs and knock on the door.

'Please, Destiny,' she said, between bangs. 'Let me in.'

I knew she wouldn't go away. I steadied myself on the side of the bath and stood up. I pulled the eye-patch back over my eye, making sure I didn't catch sight of myself in the mirror. I slid the bolt and opened the door. Ebyan and Bee were standing behind Keisha on the landing and I quickly barged past them. I didn't want to see their looks of surprise and sympathy – or worse, their shock and disgust. I fled into my bedroom. Unfortunately, there were several mirrors in there and no lock on the door. I threw myself face-down on the bed.

'We've all been so worried,' said Keisha, plonking herself down beside me. 'Aunty Dionne's going out of her mind and Uncle Alan is—'

I spun round furiously, spitting swear words and breathing fire.

'Oh, right, and I suppose you think I feel fabtastic! Give me a break, Keisha!'

'I didn't mean it like that,' said Keisha. Her chin wobbled, which made me feel even angrier. What did she have to blub about?

'So how do you really feel?' said Bee. She sat on the bed and put her arms round me in an awkward hug.

'How do you think?' I snapped, shrugging her off. 'Look at me!'

'Well, your face looks wonky,' said Bee, leaning back to look at me. 'And the pirate eye-patch doesn't really suit you.'

We all knew Bright Sparks was out of the question for me now, but Bee was the first person with enough courage to call it as she saw it. I was pleased in a way because I knew she was trying to help, but I still felt like she was stabbing me in the heart and twisting the knife.

'Even with the stupid patch, my eye is twitching,' I said. 'It keeps watering but it still feels dry. I can't eat or drink properly and everything tastes like shi— sugar!'

I paused and looked round at my friends and I felt my chest tear.

'To be honest,' I sobbed. 'I feel . . . I feel *ugly*!'

Tears were still dripping down Keisha's face, but she took my hand and gave it a squeeze. Ebyan fumbled in her bag and pulled out a couple of sheets of paper. I was surprised to see her here and I wondered how she'd managed to get out of working in the shop.

'Look at this,' she said, handing me the papers. 'I looked up Bell's Palsy and printed this out off the Internet.'

I wasn't surprised to see that Ebyan had used a high-lighter pen to mark the most important words. She had the same approach when it came to the Personal, Learning and Thinking Skills projects we got from school. I scanned the first page. Apparently, a nerve in my face had been attacked by a virus, maybe the same one that causes cold sores. This had made the nerve swell, which stopped the signals in my brain from reaching my face. Bell's Palsy was named after a Scottish surgeon called Sir Charles Bell. And, just as Dr Sunny had said, I read that it was temporary.

'It doesn't say how long though, does it?' I said gloomily. 'Temporary could mean days or weeks or even months!'

'That's true,' said Bee. 'But however long it lasts, if you have to go to school wearing an eye-patch, I think we should all do the same.'

'No way!' said Keisha. 'I so wouldn't be seen dead—'

'No way!' I said, interrupting her. 'Neither would I. I'm not going to school.'

'Have you mentioned that to Aunty Dionne and Uncle Alan?' said Keisha.

'I'm *not* going to school,' I said again. 'I'd rather eat my own spleen! Can you imagine what Bella Blake and her bully-girl mates will make of this? Even Joel Daley-Clarke wouldn't look twice at me.'

Keisha flinched. It was barely noticeable, but I suddenly realized she had a crush on him too. For months I'd been saying how much I liked him and going into meltdown whenever he was near – and she'd never said a word. It suddenly made me wonder what else she'd been keeping quiet. Maybe she was secretly planning to enter Bright Sparks as well.

'I don't care what Mum and Dad think,' I snarled, fighting back tears. 'They can't make me!'

Dad poked his head round the bedroom door. 'Think about what? Can't make you what?'

We all stared at him blankly. If anyone was going to crack, I knew it would be Ebyan. She was a terrible liar and she would never be able to keep her mouth shut like the rest of us.

'OK, girls,' said Dad, before she could say anything. 'Keep your secret. Time's up anyway. Destiny is getting upset. I think you need to leave. And before you ask, Keisha, that includes you.'

Mum and Dad didn't push it and I spent the rest of the weekend and the next couple of days watching TV, surfing the net and playing video games. I couldn't manage to play my cello because I kept drooling over the tuning pegs.

On Tuesday, after school, Keisha crash-landed into my room again.

'Hacker's on the warpath about your missed detention,' she warned. 'The only reason she hasn't called Aunty Dionne is because she still thinks you had a stroke.'

'But Mum said she phoned the school herself,' I said. 'How come Ms Hacker doesn't know I've got Bell's?'

Keisha shrugged and handed me a purple plastic document folder. 'All the other teachers seem to know,' she said. 'Mrs Obodo has sent a food technology project checklist so you don't fall too far behind. And Mr Khan has given the top set a Personal, Learning and Thinking Skills assignment but he says he hopes you get well soon. At least, I think that's what he meant. He actually said he wishes you an expeditious recuperation.'

'What's the project?' I said suspiciously, peering at her with my good eye.

'I don't think he understands about the Bell's,' warned Keisha. 'It's a cross-curriculum thing. He's following up on what he said about tattoos and piercings and linking it to that stuff we did in media studies. We have to do an essay called *Beauty and the Beast* and describe how ideas about body image and decoration have changed through history.'

'He's having a laugh,' I said. I couldn't believe it! I began to feel like the whole world had turned against me. First Bella Blake. Then Keisha. And now Mr Khan.

'You know what?' said Keisha, suddenly changing the subject. 'I don't actually think you look that bad, like. You just look as if you've been to the dentist.'

'Easy for you to say,' I snapped back. 'Why don't you think about someone else instead of yourself for once? Just imagine it, Keisha. Your whole face is numb and you can't even eat or drink properly and all your words sound funny! You look like one of the ugly sisters on a bad day and you can't play the cello without slobbering all over it! You don't have a snowflake in hell's chance of getting a boyfriend, and to top it all you've just entered a talent and beauty competition! And then you get trapped in your room doing stupid essays for stupid teachers! Have you got that in your head?'

I was angry with Mr Khan, but I was also furious with my cousin and worried that she might make a move on Joel behind my back. I couldn't stop the harsh, hateful words from tumbling out of my mouth.

Keisha's eyes widened in shock and she nodded.

'Good!' I yelled. 'Now think about it going on for

ages and not knowing when it will stop. Imagine feeling embarrassed every time you want to speak to someone. Imagine that every time you try to eat something, you dribble and drool . . .'

'I so did imagine it,' said Keisha quietly. She rummaged in her school bag. 'That's why I brought you some presents.'

'Cheese 'n' rice, Keisha, you just don't get it!' I cried. I threw myself on the bed and punched one of the pillows. 'What do I want with presents?'

'Ebyan isn't the only one who can use a computer and a highlighter pen,' said Keisha. 'These aren't just any old presents, like. I downloaded a list of things to help you get better.' She pulled something out of her bag and pushed it into my hand.

'What's this?' I said, staring down at the small green vegetable lying in the middle of my palm.

'It's the first thing on the list,' said Keisha. '*Eat a healthy, well-balanced diet rich in fruit and leafy, green vegetables.*'

I laughed and my hand flew up to cover my mouth so she wouldn't see my lips as they twisted and curled.

'So you brought me a sprig of broccoli?'

'I thought it would make you laugh,' said Keisha. 'I think it worked.'

I stared at her and my eyes filled with tears. I knew I

looked weird when I laughed. I'd stopped doing it. Losing my smile was one of the worst things about having Bell's. But losing my best friend would be worse. If anyone could see past the snarl on my face and into my heart, it was Keisha. She was the last person I should be yelling at. She was trying to cheer me up. Trying to make me feel better. The least I could do was make an effort. I uncovered my mouth and stretched it into a wonky smile.

'Thanks, cuz,' I sniffed. 'Sorry for yelling at you. You're a good friend.'

'I know,' said Keisha cheerfully. She folded her arms round me and gave me a squeeze. 'It's a shame more people don't appreciate me.'

She handed me her list, together with a brown paper bag. I peeked inside, unsure what to expect. It was a bunch of grapes – the small, green, seedless kind.

'Mum sent them,' said Keisha. 'She said they taste better than broccoli. They're healthy, bite-sized and sweet, but there's not too much juice so it won't . . . it won't . . .'

'So it won't dribble down my chin,' I said. 'Tell her I said thanks.'

'Got it in one,' said Keisha. She grinned. 'OK, what's next on the list?'

'*Number two,*' I read. '*Increase intake of vitamins B12, B6 and zinc.*'

Keisha dug around in her bag again and pulled out a box of pink, bendy drinking straws and a jar of Ovaltine chocolate-flavoured Max4Milk.

'Leftovers from Mum's cocktail party and Dad's insomnia,' said Keisha. 'He used to drink it hot like cocoa when he had trouble sleeping, but you could have it cold like milk shake. The straws will stop it . . . stop it . . .'

'Stop it dribbling down my chin!' I said, smiling as I filled in the gaps again.

'Exactamundo!' said Keisha. 'Next?'

'*Number three*,' I said, glancing back at the list. '*Exercise regularly.*'

'Oh, yes,' said Keisha. She plunged her hand back into her bag. 'The best thing would be to sign up for Halsall FC again, but I can't see you doing that any time soon so I've brought you my *Dance X-treme* workout DVD. I've brought you my *Indigo Teen Dreams* relaxation CD as well because the next thing on the list says you should reduce your stress levels. But I want them both back when you're better. OK? What's next?'

'*Practise face exercises several times a day*,' I read.

'I'll have to show you these,' said Keisha. 'I got them off YouTube. Copy me.'

She wrinkled her nose, sniffed and flared her nostrils. She curled her top lip, pressed both lips together and puckered up as if she was about to snog me. I nearly fell off the bed, partly to dodge the kiss and partly because I cracked up.

'I haven't finished yet,' she said indignantly.

She pulled her mouth into a smile and skinned her teeth. She stuck out her chin like a boxer and crinkled it. She raised her eyebrows, frowned and rubbed her cheeks in a gentle, circular motion.

'Er . . . thanks,' I muttered. 'Maybe I'll try them out later.' I glanced back at the list and felt a stab of panic. '*Six. Try acupuncture, electrical stimulation and—*'

'Stuff that!' said Keisha. 'It's jabbing pins in your face and sticking your fingers in the electric socket! What's next?'

'*Number seven,*' I said. '*Keep the face warm.*'

'Right! Bee's snow-boarding balaclava!' said Keisha.

She pulled a navy-blue and powder-pink striped fleece tube out of her bag and slipped it over my head. We both stared at my reflection in the mirror. Two drawstrings dangled at the side of my face and she pulled them tight, shrinking the hole until only my eyes were visible.

'*Superb protection from rain, snow and ice,*' she said, quoting Bee or the online catalogue she must have bought it from. No shop would be able to shift such a fashion disaster!

'She actually wears this?' I said. 'In public?'

'Only on skiing holidays with her dad and her brothers when she's sliding down snow-covered mountains, standing on a plank and stacking it as she knocks down small fir trees with her face, like,' said Keisha.

I tugged the drawstrings again until only my good eye showed and we laughed.

'Ebyan sent this as a more stylish alternative,' said Keisha, pulling a midnight-blue silk scarf from her bag. 'Hijab chic.'

She yanked off the balaclava and expertly tied the scarf round my head, draping one end across my damaged face. It clearly wasn't the first time she'd done it and it was a definite improvement on the neck gaiter. We looked in the mirror again and I noticed the subtle metallic blue stripes.

'Cooltastic!' said Keisha. She dived into her bag again. 'And this is from me,' she said, without missing a beat. Just listening to her made me feel breathless, but I looked at the glittery, pink swimming goggles she dangled in front of my nose. 'They'll keep the shampoo out of your manky eye when you wash your hair!'

'Thanks,' I said, genuinely pleased. I felt a lot better. It was great to know my friends were thinking of me, and that they cared about me – whatever I looked like.

'*Number eight. Be positive and patient,*' I read from the list. 'That's the last one.'

'Give me a break, like,' said Keisha. 'I gave you broccoli! I can't do everything. That one is down to you.'

Later, I dragged my chair across the landing to the bathroom. Then my cello. I heaved it out of the battered case and adjusted the end pin so the C peg was level with my ear. I held the cello's neck and felt its weight as I briefly rested it on my left shoulder. I placed it carefully between my knees and wriggled around until I felt comfortable. Then I gave it a hug! It was the way I checked the cello was in exactly the right position. I slipped the bow from under the bridge, tightened it and ran it lightly over the strings.

I took a deep breath and closed my eyes. I started playing a Bach cello prelude, but I improvised and wandered away from the melody and moved up and down the fingerboard. I played lots of mini-riffs, occasionally plucking and strumming the strings and slapping my hand against the backplate for rhythm.

The bathroom acoustics were great. The music vibrated in every cell of my body. It wasn't just the physical movement of tapping my fingers and the back-and-forth waving motion of my bowing arm. The music folded itself around me – inside and out. I forgot about Bell's. I floated away on the rich, warm, mellow sound that came from this huge wooden beast and just four strings. It wasn't an easy instrument to learn to play. That was part of the attraction. In primary school, I had played the recorder – but it felt like a child's toy. Playing the cello made my heart sing. I was calmer and more relaxed, but at the same time more focused and intense.

# 10

## Hell's Bells

'You can't hide out in your room for ever,' said Dad, the following weekend.

I reckon he must have me heard me playing my cello, or me and Keisha laughing, because now he'd decided that what I needed was company. And school.

'Dad,' I pleaded. 'Please don't make me go back. 'It's abuse!'

'Call Social Services,' said Dad, laughing. 'Call Childline. Call the NSPCC.'

'It's not funny,' I said glumly.

'I know,' said Dad. 'I'm deadly serious. I'm sure everyone would agree with me and your mother that you've had quite enough time off school.'

'Oh,' I said, suddenly getting it. 'This is all Mum's idea, then?'

'Listen, beautiful,' said Dad. 'We agree on this one. I have to go to Portugal on Monday and your mother has to go back to work too.'

'I don't need anyone to stay at home and look after me,' I said. 'I can fluff up pillows and microwave tomato soup for myself.'

'It's not that,' said Dad. 'We don't want you to fall any further behind with your work. And we think it's better for you to be with your friends.'

I pictured the great pile of work on my desk that Keisha had brought round, but that wasn't the biggest problem.

'You only think that because you don't know Bella Blake's boot-licking buddies,' I muttered.

'Blake?' said Dad. I wasn't sure if he'd misheard – or simply missed the point. 'Is he the boy you like?'

'He's a she,' I snapped. 'And she's a bully!'

The blood drained away from Dad's face till he was even whiter than usual.

'Don't worry,' I said quickly. I didn't want him marching into school and demanding to see the complaints procedure and the anti-bullying policy. 'I'm dealing with it.'

'Really?' said Dad. 'Are you sure?'

'Definitely,' I said.

At that moment, of course, it was a bare-faced lie,

but I suddenly decided if Bella Blake tried anything when I went back to school, I *would* deal with it. I had told Bee she needed to stand up to her and I realized I needed to follow my own advice. I smiled crookedly at Dad and snuggled in for a hug.

'By the way,' I muttered, not sure if he could hear. 'The boy I like is called Joel.'

On Monday morning, I met Keisha, Ebyan and Bee outside the Bhangra Balti House at eight-thirty for the short walk to school. I was unbelievably nervous, but after talking to Dad I was determined to get on with my life – friendships, school, cello, Bright Sparks, Joel Daley-Clarke, whatever – Bell's was not going to stop me!

'You look fine,' said Ebyan as she adjusted my scarf. 'You are like an oyster with the pearl of your beauty hidden inside.'

It sounded like she was quoting one of her favourite Somali poets. I frowned and popped a Mini-Mint.

'You just wait,' she said, clipping the corner of the scarf to my hair and wrapping it under my chin and over my head. She draped it over my damaged face and tossed the loose end over my right shoulder. 'The boys will listen to what you say instead of just eyeing you up. By this time next week, *insha'Allah*, all the girls will be wearing scarves.'

She grinned at me and I smiled back. The scarf was beautiful, but it did nothing for my confidence. I felt self-conscious, and Bella Blake spotted us as soon as we walked through the school gates. She swaggered across the playground with her latest batch of mates. Madison and Ashleigh were still there but she had rounded up a few more sheep.

'Oooh, look,' she sneered. 'It's Ali Baba's babes.'

'How long did it take you to think of that?' said Ebyan. 'You must have been up all night.'

Ebyan usually ignored idiots like Bella so I was impressed when she spoke up to defend us. She strolled away with her shoulders back and her head held high and I followed her example and scurried after her.

As we filed into our form room, I noticed Mrs Obodo was a bit thrown by the sight of me wearing a hijab. But her main concern seemed to be whether it fitted in with regulation school uniform because it wasn't plain navy blue.

'Pop in to get it approved by Mrs Parveen at break time, please, Destiny,' she said. 'Oh, yes, and that reminds me, Ms Hacker wants to see you at break time too.'

My heart sank. I'd only been back in school five minutes and I was already in trouble.

'And by the way, Destiny, welcome back. It's good

to see you looking so well,' added Mrs Obodo, lying smoothly.

Mrs Obodo took the register and collected in the food technology projects. A few kids hadn't finished theirs or had forgotten to bring them in. Jack Cooper said he couldn't find anyone to copy from and Omar Hussein said his baby sister had eaten his, after smearing it with mango chutney. I'd spent most of Saturday finishing mine and I was feeling pretty pleased with myself until we got to history just after break time.

'Where's your PLTS project?' said Mr Khan.

'Our broadband connection was down so I couldn't do any research,' I said. I sounded even less convincing than Omar Hussein and Mrs Obodo. 'Then the computer crashed and I lost it.'

'What an unfortunate and calamitous tale of woe,' said Mr Khan. 'Don't fret, Destiny. You can come to the library for an after-school detention a week on Thursday. You can learn how people used reference books for research and wrote essays by hand, back in the good old days.'

'*Next* Thursday?' I said, checking. 'Not this Thursday?'

'That's right,' said Mr Khan. 'I believe you already have a detention with Ms Hacker this week.'

I groaned. He was right. I don't know how I'd

forgotten. Ms Hacker had left me in no doubt about what would happen if I missed her detention again. She had made it crystal clear the only alternative really was execution by firing squad!

This whole day was going from bad to worse, although because I had spent most of break time traipsing around school looking for teachers, at least I hadn't bumped into Bella Blake again. And Mrs Parveen had examined the barely visible metallic stripes on my scarf and decided they were acceptable.

To be honest, though, I began to feel like I was just drawing more attention to myself by wearing it. A few kids asked me if I'd converted to Islam after my near-death experience a couple of weeks ago and some wondered if I was making a fashion statement. The scarf kept the breeze off my face, but it didn't hide the damage and I began to wonder whether wearing it had been a mistake. Who was I kidding? Coming back to school at all had been the real mistake!

I found a quiet corner in the library to eat my lunch. My sense of taste was gradually returning to normal and nothing tasted anywhere near as bad as that Bizarre Bar when I first got Bell's. But I was still struggling to eat and drink and I didn't even want my friends to see me slurping soup and yoghurt, then sucking blackcurrant juice through a straw. Besides, Bell's had affected my hearing too. I was sensitive to noise and I needed a break from the hustle and bustle of the canteen and the playground.

I decided to start reading stuff for my history project. The first thing I found out was that the perfect body shape ranged from plump and curvy to skinny and flat-chested in different cultures and at different times in history. In the past, there had been some excruciating – and sometimes fatal – ideas about beauty, like corsets that scrunched your internal organs, poisonous lead face powder, foot-binding, neck-stretching, crocodile-poo mud-baths and mouse-skin eyebrows. Yuck! Even these days, everyone is weaving and waxing, and wearing false nails, eyelashes, boobs and teeth. Mum had warned me not to compare myself to the fake, airbrushed pictures of super-skinny models and over-botoxed celebs in magazines and online. She was always telling me how important it was for girls to separate how they look from how they feel. But if I added Bell's to the mix, it was impossible.

I was so wrapped up in reading about how some cultures cut the skin in decorative patterns to leave permanent scars that I didn't notice Bella and her evil crones until they were standing right in front of me. The shock made me cough and splutter and I watched in horror as masses of tiny purple blackcurrant juice stains spread across the pages of the encyclopaedia and down the front of my blouse.

'Hell's bells,' I muttered under my breath.

'Hello, freak-show,' sneered Bella. 'Not so pretty any more, are you?'

The other girls snorted and sniggered, but I forced myself to keep my head up and meet Bella's stony, grey-eyed gaze.

'You're so ugly, you make onions cry,' said Ashleigh.

'You're so ugly, your doctor is a vet,' said Madison.

They were so lame, I nearly laughed out loud. Was that the best they could do? I popped a Mini-Mint, gathered up my stuff and started to walk away.

'Be careful if you're going out to the playground,' said Bella. 'You'll frighten the Year Sevens without even saying boo!'

'Keep talking, Bella,' I said, over my shoulder. 'You never know, one day you might say something friendly or intelligent.'

'Like Joel Daley-Clarke, you mean?' said Bella.

I felt like she'd thrown a bucket of icy water over me. I stopped walking and turned round.

'I knew that would get your attention.' Bella's eyes gleamed. 'I heard him talking about you to his mates. Do you want to know what he said?'

I shivered. It was a trick question – and I didn't know the right answer. Had she really heard him? And even if she had, would she tell me?

'Well?' said Bella with a sly smile. 'Do you want to know or not?'

If I said yes, she'd probably want me to get down on my knees and beg.

'No thanks,' I said firmly.

I walked round the end of the non-fiction and reference bookshelves, but Bella's voice rang out and shattered the quiet stillness of the library.

'He said he never fancied you much to begin with, but kissing you now would be like kissing a box of frogs!' she yelled. 'He said he wouldn't kiss you if you were the last girl on the planet. He said he'd rather drown in a bucket of vomit!'

I broke into a run, but the tears streamed down my face before I even made it to the door.

After three days of non-stop name-calling, insults and threats, I realized that Bella's ultimate goal was to completely rob me of any confidence and totally destroy my self-esteem. If I was honest, she was making a good job of it. At first, I gave as good as I got. I called her a few choice names of my own. I stopped wearing my scarf and tried to tough it out. But gradually I noticed I was walking with my head down, hiding my face and turning into a complete loser. I felt worse than when I first started high school and didn't know anyone and hadn't made any friends. This was how Bee must have felt when everyone was dissing her.

On the fourth day, while I was in detention with Ms Hacker, Bella sent me a text message which simply said: *Box of frogs!* She was mean and bitchy but she wasn't stupid. We both knew there was no way I would be able to persuade Mrs Parveen or my parents that the text had anything to do with cyber-bullying.

I wondered how Bella even knew my number. Maybe she'd ambushed Bee in the toilets again and beaten it out of her. Maybe she'd caught Keisha off-guard on the way home and bribed her with the information that she was in with more of a chance with Joel after what he'd said about me. Or maybe she'd gone to Suuqa Samiira to see Ebyan and simply asked her.

A part of me knew I'd lost the plot. The girls who hung around with Bella only did it because they thought that if they sucked up to her enough, they wouldn't end up being targeted. I knew my friends had more sense than that. But that didn't stop me going home and crying into my pillow because the other part of me wondered if Bella had been right – and that no one liked me with a mashed-up face.

The next day, in Friday assembly, Bella was sitting a few chairs along from me. She leaned forward and smacked her lips and pretended to blow me kisses. I realized she would never stop tormenting me unless I could beat her at her own nasty game. I would have to gang up with Bee and all her other past victims. We would have to bully Bella like she had bullied us. I would have to turn Ashleigh and Madison against her. I would have to get her to believe she was a useless nobody. It would never work, I thought grimly. It would take ages and I didn't have the patience. Or the time.

I swallowed hard and struggled to hold back the tears, which stung my eyes and threatened to spill down my cheeks. The next time Bella pouted at me and made that disgusting *mwagh-mwagh* noise, I clenched my fists. I looked into her narrowed, hate-filled eyes and gritted my teeth on the good side of my mouth. I imagined myself slapping the evil grin off her face. I pictured myself landing a perfect upper-cut that shut her mouth, followed by a well-aimed drop-kick that left her lying on the floor, quiet and still.

Suddenly, I realized I was going to do it! I leaped up, knocking over my chair, and charged towards her. Some of the girls around me screamed in shock. Even the lads looked surprised. Bella saw me coming. She must have seen the fiery rage and violent intent in my eyes. She sprang up, ready to fight me off, but she lost her balance. Her knees buckled. She wobbled and swayed in slow motion before she fell heavily onto the floor and gave everyone in our year group a full-on flash of her grey granny knickers! For a second or two, she didn't move. But as the sniggers grew in volume and became a chorus of loud, raucous laughs, Bella's face flushed deep red. She clutched at her skirt, yanking it down over her mottled thighs and scrambled shakily to her feet. She ran out of the hall, screeching and squealing in protest like a scalded cat.

# 11

## Lucky Stars

Two hours later, I was still sitting outside Mrs Parveen's office, waiting for Mum and Dad. Dad was catching an earlier flight all the way from Lisbon and Mum had hopped into a mini-cab from the Bullring in the centre of town. I prayed for a miracle, hoping Dad would arrive first.

There was a steady stream of teachers in and out of the office as Mrs Parveen tried to get to the bottom of what she described as my vicious and totally un-provoked attack. I'm sure the conversations were meant to be private, but in the odd moments when the school secretary wasn't bellowing down the phone, using the printer or shredder or doing something else equally noisy, snippets of what they were saying about me drifted through the paper-thin wall.

'Worked hard to catch up . .' said Mrs Obodo. 'Just standing up . . .'

'Always plenty of . . .' said Mr Khan. 'She has the potential to . . .'

'Non-stop trouble,' said Ms Hacker. 'Permanent execution . . . I mean, exclusion!'

It was hard to fill in the gaps, but until Ms Hacker got started I reckon most of them thought I was a model pupil who would definitely go far!

Mum arrived first and completely surprised me. She threw her arms round me in a protective hug and demanded to see a copy of the complaints procedure and anti-bullying policy. She had spoken to Dad on the phone and he had obviously told her all about Bella. Mum was furious nothing had been done to stop Bella picking on me, especially since my face had been scrambled.

But none of what Mum or my teachers said made any difference. I hadn't actually laid a finger on Bella, but as far as Mrs Parveen was concerned I had broken the school rules – again – and she excluded me for three days.

'You can thank your lucky stars it's not permanent,' she said as Mum and I left her office.

In the corridor, I popped a Mini-Mint. Mum pressed her lips together and knotted her eyebrows into a frown. I wasn't quite sure if she was fed up with me or annoyed about the total unfairness of my punishment.

Dad arrived home soon after we did. He gave me a quick hug and immediately sent me to my room while he and Mum discussed what to do with me. Our walls and doors were thicker than the ones at school. I couldn't hear what they were saying, but ever since I was a toddler they had told me not to hit or bite or kick back – except on the soccer pitch – and they had taught me that violence doesn't solve anything. It wasn't exactly the biggest shock in the world when they grounded me.

To be honest, I wasn't bothered about not being able to go out. It was hard to deal with kids staring and making random comments about my face – and sometimes adults were even worse. But Mum and Dad also took away my TV, my computer and even my phone!

I spent most of Saturday finishing my history project and most of Sunday practising random cello solos even though I knew I wasn't going to be performing at Bright Sparks.

In the evening, I realized that my head had stopped feeling like soggy mashed potato and there was a tingly sensation in my face and ear. I was dribbling less and my words weren't so mangled, but I tried not to get my hopes up. Keisha's sprig of broccoli still sat on my windowsill, reminding me to be patient and positive, but it was yellow and wrinkled and looked as tired and sorry for itself as I was.

Keisha, Ebyan and Bee came round after school on Monday while Mum and Dad were still at work. They were bursting with news.

'You're a hero!' said Keisha before she was even through the door. 'Everyone's totally impressed that someone had the guts to stand up to Bella.'

'We all had to write a report for Mrs Parveen,' said Ebyan.

'Even Ashleigh and Madison said it wasn't your fault,' said Bee. 'They admitted Bella was to blame.'

'I think they took the chance to get shot of her, like,' said Keisha.

'And keep themselves out of trouble,' I added bitterly.

'I heard from Bright Sparks,' said Bee, changing the subject abruptly. 'I haven't made it to the live final.'

'Oh, Bee,' I said, disappointed. 'What a shame. I'm so sorry.'

'Am I bothered?' said Bee. 'Nah! It was fun and just entering kept Mum happy. And we've been shopping without my brothers to buy make-up and a few more girly clothes. It was a good experience, but I'm glad I don't have to see it through to the end.'

'What about you?' said Keisha, giving me an odd look. 'Did you get through to the final, like?'

'No idea,' I said. 'Mum and Dad nabbed every means of communication. I've had no contact with the outside world all weekend. I haven't been able to check my email.'

'Let's have a look now,' said Bee, pulling out her snazzy e-phone.

'What's the point?' I said, suddenly coming to my senses and pulling myself together. 'Who cares? There's no way I'm parading up and down a stage when I still look like the back of a bus!'

'You do not!' said Keisha. 'Anyway, you can play the cello without dribbling now and you can definitely give a talk and answer a few questions.'

'We have to tell her the truth!' said Ebyan, interrupting. 'I am sorry, Destiny. I hacked into your email account. They made me!'

'Everyone at school already knows that you entered Bright Sparks,' said Keisha. 'Everyone has been texting or logging on to the website to vote for you.'

'Everyone?' I said. All except Bella Blake and Joel Daley-Clarke, I bet. 'How did they find out?'

'Well, I did tell a few people when we first entered

and it just spread from there,' admitted Bee. 'But it's not all bad news,' she added anxiously. 'You made it. You're in the final!'

I shook my head in disbelief. I was as far away from beautiful as it was possible to be – and now the whole school knew I had entered a beauty contest! Maybe Mum had been right all along. Who cared if it was a beauty contest with a twist?

'What the hell is the matter with you?' I demanded, looking at each of them in turn. 'You're all crazy if you think I'm going anywhere near Bright Sparks.'

'Why not?' said Bee. 'You're not going to let Bell's get the better of you, are you?'

'There's no pressure,' said Keisha, ignoring her. 'We so understand if you've changed your mind and you don't want to go through with it, like.'

'No, we don't,' said Bee.

'Yes, we do!' said Keisha. She glared at Bee and turned to me. 'Ebyan was right, cuz. Even if you are brainy and talented, you still have to look a certain way for this sort of thing. Let's be honest, like, and face facts. You don't stand much chance of winning.'

I didn't know what to say. I was scared she was right. But I was shocked that my friends were arguing about me.

'That's rubbish,' snarled Bee, turning on Keisha. 'And you're full of it!'

Keisha's face clouded. 'And who exactly asked you?' she hissed, which sounded worse than if she'd been shouting. 'Who made *Betty Bucket* the expert on *presentation and poise*?' She spat the last few words, knowing they would hit home.

There was a long beat of silence and Bee's eyes flooded with tears. 'I'm never going to be part of your cosy little clique, am I?' she said sadly. She picked up her bag and we watched her shuffle across the room, then listened as she padded down the stairs.

'What?' snapped Keisha, when we heard the front door close.

'That was a bit harsh,' I said.

'I was standing up for you,' said Keisha.

'I know but—'

'Stuff it, then!' said Keisha, cutting me off. 'I've had a bellyful of this! I'm so sick of Bell's, anyone would think I had it myself. Why have a go at me when I'm just trying to help? If I tell you that you look OK, you don't believe me. If I tell you that you don't look good enough to win a beauty competition, you don't believe that either.'

She snatched up her own bag and barged past me. She stomped down the stairs and slammed the front door. I found myself shaking. I looked at Ebyan.

'I had better go after her,' she said quietly. 'She is my best friend. I cannot help with your decision, Destiny. You are the only one who can decide.'

Amongst the bills and junk mail waiting for Mum and Dad when they came home from work, there was a big A4 envelope addressed to me. There was also a letter from school for Mum and Dad. Luckily for me, Mum was so focused on that, she didn't see the Bright Sparks logo or the *DO NOT BEND* sticker on my envelope and I smuggled it upstairs without her noticing.

Mum and Dad's letter confirmed some of what my so-called friends had already told me. After she had finished her investigation, Mrs Parveen agreed that Bella had been provoking me but she still did not approve of my response. Bella had been excluded for five days and Mrs Parveen said the school would try to give her help with changing her bullying behaviour.

I didn't give a flying fig! I was already certain that Bella Blake would never bother me again. But not having enemies was nothing compared to not having friends.

After dinner, I opened the Bright Sparks envelope. There was a printed *WITH COMPLIMENTS* slip and six large, glossy photographs. I spread them out on my bed and stared at them.

The girl who looked back at me was beautiful. There was a golden glow to her light-brown skin and her eyes were shining. She smiled out, radiant and happy. I burst into tears.

She was so pretty.

And I was so ugly.

It was impossible to believe the girl in the pictures was me.

# 12

## Bright Sparks

I went back to school again on Thursday. I didn't bother to wait for my so-called friends outside the Bhangra Balti House, which turned out to be a good decision. When I saw them later, Keisha and Ebyan put their heads together and started whispering and Bee pretended she hadn't even seen me. Nothing Bella Blake had ever done to me made me feel as bad as I felt right then. I told myself I didn't care, but I wasn't sure how I made it through the day. And at the end of it, I still had detention with Mr Khan. I gave him my essay, and while he read it, I sneaked a quick peek at my email on the library computer.

The Bright Sparks message sat in my inbox like a bad joke. I was one of the twenty finalists. The event would take place at the International Convention Centre in

Broad Street this coming Saturday. I gazed into space and daydreamed about whether I might have won if Mum wasn't a bitter has-been and my ex-friends had any idea how to be supportive – and, of course, if I hadn't had my face destroyed by Bell's!

'Excellent essay,' said Mr Khan, breaking into my thoughts. 'You are right about how quickly we form opinions of people based on appearance – and you have a good understanding of the different historical and cultural views of beauty.'

I shrugged. 'I understand that beauty comes in all colours and shapes and sizes,' I said gloomily. 'But I'm sure wonky faces never did it for anyone, whatever century they lived in or whatever country they came from.'

'Do you think I need to set you another PLTS project?' said Mr Khan. 'About how beauty is . . .?'

'. . . in the eye of the beholder!' I said quickly, cutting him off. 'No thanks, Mr Khan. I get it! Beauty is more than skin deep.'

'Indubitably,' said Mr Khan, which I think meant he agreed with me.

All that evening and the next day, I could think of nothing else except the Bright Sparks competition. Somehow, since I got Bell's, I had let myself get sucked in by the beauty part of the contest and I'd forgotten all about the rest. But the truth was I *could* still answer questions and play my cello, whatever I looked like. I *could* still be spotted by a music industry A & R talent-scout. I *could* still be offered a major record deal! OK, it was unlikely, but it definitely wasn't going to happen if I stayed at home and hid under the duvet.

On Saturday morning, I sneaked out of the house while Mum and Dad were still asleep. I folded my retro-print sundress into my rucksack and took my cello, my talent and my brains into town on the bus.

I walked across Centenary Square to Broad Street and looked up at the blue-tinted windows and white stone of the International Convention Centre. The Symphony Hall was in the same building, and for a second, I had a vision of myself, some time in the future, arriving here for my debut cello recital.

I popped a Mini-Mint and yanked myself back to the present. I made my way past an Italian restaurant to the central mall, where a group of over-excited mothers were sizing up each other's daughters. They traded admiring or dirty looks as they instantly decided who might be borderline competition or a real threat to their chances of winning the Bright Sparks competition. They did a double take when they looked in my direction and noticed my lop-sided face, but they glanced away quickly, already sure I couldn't possibly be a finalist. I muttered insults at them under my breath but I sashayed past them with my shoulders pulled back and my head held high.

Maybe my own mother had been right. So far, every round of the competition had been based on looks – on fluttering and flaunting – whatever the rules said about talent and brains. If I'd had Bell's when I first entered, I would never have got this far!

I threaded my way to the registration desk. A tall, elegant woman with cropped, silver hair was handing out T-shirts emblazoned with the Bright Sparks logo, wristbands with contestant numbers and copies of the day's schedule.

'Welcome to the Bright Sparks final,' she said, stretching her orange lipstick-covered mouth into a wide smile, but not quite meeting my eye. 'I'm Lucia Torino, the executive director. The group press photo will be here in the foyer in a few minutes.' She frowned in the direction of my cello case as if it was a coffin. 'You have just enough time to hang up your clothes and drop off your . . . er . . . props, but I need you back here pronto.'

I followed her directions to the changing room. A few girls were ogling themselves in the long row of mirrors and putting the finishing touches to their hair and make-up, and thankfully no one noticed me. I wasn't surprised. I had prepared myself for being stared at or ignored – and for the nasty comments I knew would come. But even though I was uncomfortable, I was determined to go through with the competition whatever happened. I had a point to prove – to my mother, to my so-called friends and to myself: I was a talented musician and so much more than just a pretty face.

I popped a Mini-Mint and glanced down at the schedule:

| | |
|---|---|
| 9:00 | Registration |
| 9:15 | Press photographs |
| 9:30 | Speeches |
| 10:30 | Break and optional costume change |
| 11:00 | Interviews |
| 12:30 | Lunch and optional costume change |
| 14:00 | Performances |
| 15:30 | Interval and costume change |
| 16:00 | Procession and pageant |
| 17:00 | Bright Sparks Award ceremony |
| 18:00 | Press interviews |

Just reading it made me feel overwhelmed, but I pulled on the T-shirt, fluffed up my hair and re-applied my lip gloss. I curled my lashes but decided against mascara because it just drew attention to my wonky eye.

Back in the foyer, Flor and a couple of photographers from the *Mail* and the *Post* were setting up their cameras and Lucia Torino was organizing everyone into number order. She skilfully manoeuvred me towards the back of the group, even though my wristband number was three. It probably wasn't a bad thing. If Mum spotted the picture in the paper, perhaps she wouldn't even notice me.

After the photos, we moved on to one of the conference rooms and I recognized Miss Bitchy Boots from Flor's studio. She stared hard at my face.

'What are you looking at?' I snapped, using the same unfriendly tone she'd used on me and Bee.

'I dunno,' she said, quick as a flash. 'The label must have fell off.'

I turned away, suddenly lost for words and unable to find a come-back.

'If she wins this thing, it's rigged,' said Miss Bitchy Boots to the girl next to her, but loud enough for everyone to hear. 'It's a fix.'

I expected the other girl to snigger in agreement, but she glanced at me and smiled nervously. I popped another Mini-Mint and looked around the auditorium.

There was a full-size stage with blue velvet curtains and a catwalk between rows and rows of blue chairs for the audience. I followed the other contestants to the seats just behind the panel of judges and waited for my name to be called so I could introduce myself and give my short speech.

When it was my turn, I walked up the steps at the front of the stage and tried to compose myself. I ran through my preparation in my head – be loud, be clear, be confident, smile and don't fidget.

'Good morning, ladies and gentlemen – and fellow contestants,' I began. 'My name is Destiny Buckley-Reid and I attend Halsall High School. My favourite subjects are music, history and PE. I'm planning to rejoin Halsall Football Club and my future ambition is to be a professional musician.'

I tried to smile and turn up my volume.

'I would like to talk about the idea that beauty is more than skin deep. When I first entered Bright Sparks, I looked normal. I know it's hard to believe, but I was even prettier than some of you.' It was meant to be a joke but no one laughed. 'Then I got Bell's Palsy, and that's why I look like this.'

I paused to give everyone enough time to look at me, now I had given them my permission. I could feel my heart hammering in my chest. I tried to steady my breathing, and when I trusted my voice not to wobble I started speaking again.

'Even though some people thought I was pretty, I don't think I was big-headed about it. And even though I entered this competition, I don't want to be a model or anything. I want to be a musician. But with Bell's Palsy, it's hard to think about anything else except your looks. I'm always wondering how people will react. I'm always wishing I had my old face back.'

I took another big breath. I had no idea how my talk was going down, because I could hardly see the audience even out of my good eye. The spotlight was almost blinding me.

'Bell's has knocked my confidence too,' I went on. 'It's even made me push away my friends, which is why I'm here on my own. But I wanted to come here today to prove I still have the talent, brains and personality that the Bright Sparks judges are looking for – and that's why I still deserve to win.'

From her judge's chair, Lucia Torino gave me a quick nod. Behind her, the other contestants and their parents and friends gave a polite round of applause. As I left the stage, I missed having my own crowd of supporters like everyone else. But during the break, I realized my speech must have gone well enough to worry some of the other girls because someone had smeared mascara all down the front of my sundress. I changed into it anyway, ready for the interview section of the competition. We had to answer one question each and they were picked at random out of a hat.

'What has been your most significant accomplishment?'

'At what point does a girl become a woman?'

'What makes a good friend?'

Luckily, that was my question. I didn't even need to think about it.

'Loyalty, honesty and respect,' I said quickly. 'And someone who will let you borrow their jeans,' I added, with only the faintest hint of a slur.

At lunch time, the girl who had smiled at me earlier invited me to sit at the same table. I wondered if she was alone too, but I was wrong. All her family and half her school had come along to support her. After a few minutes, I made an excuse and went to sit with my cello in the changing room and dribble juice in private.

I thought about giving up and going home, but I gritted my teeth and hung on until the talent part of the competition. I was one of the last performers and I had decided to play my own variations on the Allegro from the *Sonata in E minor, Opus 1, number 2* by Benedetto Marcello.

Sitting alone in the centre of the stage, I raised my

bow and wished with all my heart that Keisha, Ebyan and Bee were in the audience. I couldn't pretend any more that it was OK being on my own. I was sad and lonely – and angry! My bow arm trembled and I dropped it to my side. What was the point? I was kidding myself. I had zero chance of winning Bright Sparks – or being talent-spotted – and no one here even cared if I lived or died!

'Get on with it!' cried a woman's voice from the audience.

Oh, great, I thought miserably. And now I'm being heckled! I had the impression that the audience was bigger than for the morning programme, but the spotlight still dazzled me and made my wonky eye water. It was difficult to make out any faces.

'Come on, bab!' yelled the woman. 'Don't just sit there looking pretty!'

I stared out, over the heads of the judges – and gradually, far away in the back row of the auditorium, Mrs Hagley's pale, papery face emerged from the darkness. As I squinted, I realized with a shock that Mum, Dad, Uncle Devon and Aunty Esme were sitting next to her on one side, and Keisha, Ebyan, Bee and Mrs Buchet were sitting on the other! They must have just arrived – but how did any of them even know I was here?

I shuddered as I had a sudden vision of Mrs Hagley

hanging her washing out on the line and gossiping with Mum over the garden wall. It was my own fault. Mrs Hagley had told me to tell Mum about the Bright Sparks malarkey ages ago. She didn't know it was still supposed to be a secret. Mum must have told Dad, of course, and then she must have phoned Aunty Esme and Uncle Devon too! It was a chain, and the next link led to Keisha, then Ebyan and Bee – and finally even to Mrs Buchet. I wasn't sure if I felt relieved or terrified but I raised my bow again and began to play.

My heartbeat and my breathing immediately slowed and I felt a tingling sensation on the back of my neck. I melted into the music and let it carry me away.

As well as my family and friends, Mrs Hagley must have told half the neighbours in our street that I was in the Bright Sparks final – and Bee must have told half the kids from school. From the cheering, whooping and deafening applause that followed my performance, I reckoned most of them had come along to support me. And – to my absolute gob-smacked amazement – I saw that Joel Daley-Clarke was one of them!

I made the most of it and took several curtain calls. I realized I didn't need to win the competition to feel like a winner. I was proud of myself just for showing up and taking part and I tried not to think about the trouble I'd be in when Mum got hold of me. To be honest, I half expected her to come and drag me off the stage and make an embarrassing scene and I was relieved when I managed to slide safely back into my seat to watch the last few talent performances.

After a tragic magic act, a brilliant signed song and an impressive rhythmic gymnastics routine, the judges huddled together to decide the overall winners. Some of the other contestants got up and went to sit with their families, but I stayed put and tried to decide whether anyone on the panel looked like a music industry talent scout.

Of course, I knew I wasn't going to win, but when the judges had completed their deliberations and Lucia Torino finally took to the stage, I still found myself crossing my fingers and toes. She made a speech and rambled on for a while about how Bright Sparks was different from other competitions because it valued and encouraged other qualities in girls besides their looks, such as confidence and self-esteem, public speaking and performance skills.

I could just imagine Mum's reaction to all that. She was probably spitting feathers and I glanced round quickly to check. Dad's face was beaming with happiness and pride but Mum's was folded into a thin-lipped snarl.

I turned back to the stage and listened and watched

in horror as Lucia Torino announced that the Miss Bright Sparks Beauty winner was . . . Miss Bitchy Boots! But her prize was a tacky tiara, a trashy sash and a bucket-load of cosmetics and fake tan. It served her right!

After the main presentation and press photographs, the judges awarded a few far more useful prizes like a Performing Arts summer school course for Miss Bright Sparks Talent.

'And last but not least,' announced Lucia Torino, 'the prize of thirty pounds in book tokens for Miss Bright Sparks Brains goes to . . . Destiny Buckley-Reid.'

I collected my gold envelope in a state of total shock, and as I staggered back down the steps Keisha, Ebyan and Bee rushed over and hugged me.

'You were brill, cuz,' said Keisha.

'*Félicitations*,' said Bee, which was French for roughly the same thing.

'Your playing was wonderful,' said Ebyan. 'And your friendship is a blessing.'

I hugged them back, and over Ebyan's shoulder I saw Mum's face light up with the faintest glimmer of a smile.

# BELL'S PALSY

Bell's Palsy is a temporary weakness or paralysis of the muscles on one side of the face which can also affect the eye. It usually affects people between the ages of 15 and 40 years but it is quite rare.

The exact cause of Bell's Palsy is unknown, although many doctors think the facial nerve is attacked by the same virus that causes cold sores.

The symptoms, which can develop very quickly, include:

• drooping or sagging mouth
• inability to close the eye
• dryness in the eye
• watering eye
• pain underneath the ear
• altered sense of taste
• sensitivity to noise
• drooling

Doctors don't always agree about the treatment but most prescribe eye drops and an eye patch to protect the eye.

It's important to take care of yourself, to eat well and get plenty of sleep when you have Bell's Palsy. The facial nerve takes time to heal but most people start to improve within a few weeks and almost all make a full recovery within a few months.

For further information you can visit these sites:

http://www.cks.nhs.uk/patient_information_leaflet/bells_palsy
http://www.bellspalsy.org.uk

# STROKE

A stroke happens when the supply of blood to the brain is cut off. The brain is damaged because of a lack of oxygen.

Most strokes happen to people over the age of 65. Strokes in children and young adults are extremely rare – when it does happen they are usually related to infections or other health problems.

The effects of a stroke will depend on which part of the brain is not able to work properly. Children heal better than adults because their nervous system and brain are more flexible. With the help of physiotherapy and speech therapy, most children make a full recovery.

The symptoms of stroke are similar in children and adults:

• severe headache
• speech difficulties
• eye movement problems
• numbness and or paralysis in one side of the body

By recognizing the symptoms and acting fast, you can help doctors reduce any damage to the brain.

Use the following to help you think **F.A.S.T.**

| FACE | Ask the child to smile.<br>Does one side of the face droop? |
|------|-------------------------------------------------------------|
| ARMS | Ask the child to raise both arms.<br>Does one arm drift downward? |
| SPEECH | Ask the child to repeat a simple sentence.<br>Are the words slurred? Can the patient repeat the sentence correctly? |
| TIME | If the child shows any of these symptoms, time is important.<br>Call 999 or get to the hospital fast. Brain cells are dying. |

http://www.childstrokesupport.com
http://www.differentstrokes.co.uk

# Beastly Beauty

- Stick-on beauty spots were originally used to cover up smallpox scars

- In ancient Egypt, men, women and children outlined their eyelids with kohl eyeliner to make themselves beautiful, reduce the glare of the desert, repel flies and to protect them from the 'Evil Eye'

- The ancient Egyptians also used crushed gemstones like lapis lazuli or green malachite to decorate their eyelids

- Some people believe that massaging your body with your own pee (urine) leaves your skin feeling soft and smooth

- The ancient Romans used pee as a mouthwash to whiten their teeth and freshen their breath

- Snail mucus is used to reduce acne scars, prevent sun damage and wrinkles

- Fish pedicures use little black 'Doctor Fish' (Garra Rufa) to nibble the old, flaky skin on your feet and toes to leave them soft, smooth and beautiful

- Bird poo (faeces) from nightingales was used by Japanese geishas and kabuki actors to wipe the heavy, white makeup off their faces and today and today a sterilised bird poo facial is believed to bring a translucent glow to your face

- Ancient beauty treatments contained some very strange and/or dangerous ingredients like crocodile poo, arsenic and lead

- Modern cosmetics also contain some weird ingredients including salt (sodium chloride), pepper (oleoresin capsicum), egg white (albumen), fish scales, cochineal (an extract of carminic acid from squished female scale insects) and plastic

# Sugar and Spice Quiz

## What Kind of Friend are You?

**1. I am...**

a) enthusiastic and emotional

b) clever and confident

c) caring and creative

d) responsible and reliable

**2. My friends think I am...**

a) funny and up for a laugh

b) determined and up for a challenge

c) energetic and up for adventure

d) easy-going and up for anything

**3. When I talk to other people I am...**

a) chatty and often change my opinion

b) decisive and make up my mind quickly

c) sensitive to other people's point of view

d) good at listening and like to hear other people's ideas

**4. People like me because I am...**

a) dramatic and friendly

b) realistic and practical

c) artistic and helpful

d) sympathetic and generous

**5. My best qualities are my...**

a) leadership and passion

b) ambition and confidence

c) imagination and concern for others

d) relaxed attitude and flexibility

## 6. When I plan things I like to......

a) decide what I want at the time

b) sort things out in detail and in advance

c) make group decisions

d) let other people decide

## 7. When things need to get done I like to...

a) work in a team and be in charge

b) do it myself to make sure it's done right

c) discuss new ways of doing things

d) share ideas and make sure everyone is happy

## 8. My life motto is...

a) keep smiling

b) do it now

c) reach for the stars

d) go with the flow

## 9. I am full of...

a) life

b) confidence

c) ideas

d) patience

## 10. I would like to be less...

a) messy

b) bossy

c) moody

d) lazy

## Mostly As: Miss/Mr Popularity

You like other people and you make friends easily

You are always up for new things and the life and soul of any party

You are creative and colourful

You don't hold grudges and you apologize quickly

## Mostly Bs: Miss/Mr Independent

You are self-sufficient and don't need to lean on your friends

You like to be right – and you usually are

You are very confident and focused on your goals

You are a born leader and organiser and you work well in groups

## Mostly Bs: Miss/Mr Creativity

You make friends slowly and carefully but you are very loyal and reliable

You don't really like being the centre of attention

You are talented and creative and may be musical and/or artistic

You are a good listener and you care for other people

## Mostly Ds: Miss/Mr Adaptability

You get on well with other people and you have lots of friends

You are easygoing and relaxed

You are sympathetic and kind

You are a good listener and you are able to sort out problems

# Also available
# from Tamarind Books...

# Tamarind biography series

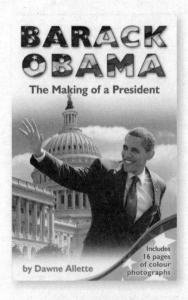

"*The inspirational story of an inspirational man, very well written, presented in a really accessible manner and a real joy to read.*" *Malorie Blackman*

Also available
Michelle Obama

 **Biographies of black British icons for 9+ years**

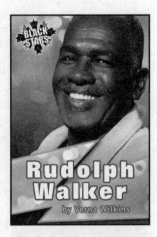

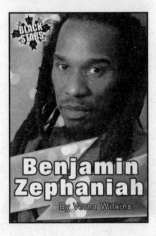

To see the rest of our list, please visit our website:

www.tamarindbooks.co.uk

On the dusty fields of Zimbabwe, Deo finds meaning in football. He's a Man United fan with a home-made ball and one day he's going to make it big.

Innocent, his older brother, isn't like the other boys; he's slow sometimes, but no one dares say so – not with Deo watching.

When the soldiers come with their trail of death and destruction, the boys have no choice but to flee for their lives. Deo stuffs his football with billions of worthless dollars and leads his brother on the long road to South Africa in search of safety.

A raw, beautiful and moving story of two brothers on a transformative journey that will stick with the readers long after the last page.

ISBN 9781848530836

# How to Save a DRAGON

Oscar can't believe his ears when Ferris Fleet tells
him that dragons aren't just fairy-tales, but it's
true: dragons are really real, and hundreds once
called World Nine home.

But that was before the Dragon-Chasers came;
before they hunted down almost every dragon alive
to steal their eggs and their gleaming rainbow
skin. Now Fleet and his friends are doing
everything they can to protect what few remain.

Oscar wants to help – and he may just get
his chance. Because a stranger's arrived in
Lonelyheart – a man who gives Oscar the creeps.
A man they say is a hunter and a poacher, a
man who wears a coat of gleaming rainbows . . .

By Annie Dalton
Illustrated By Carl Pearce
ISBN 9781848530478